Bases Loaded

LISA SUZANNE

BASES LOADED
VEGAS HEAT: BASES LOADED
BOOK FOUR
© LISA SUZANNE 2024

All rights reserved. In accordance with the US Copyright Act of 1976, the scanning, uploading, and sharing of any part of this book without the permission of the publisher or author constitute unlawful piracy and theft of the author's intellectual property. No part of this book may be reproduced or transmitted in any form or by any means, electronic or mechanical, including photocopying, recording, or by any information storage and retrieval system without the written permission of the author, except where permitted by law and except for excerpts used in reviews. If you would like to use any words from this book other than for review purposes, prior written permission must be obtained from the publisher.

Published in the United States of America by Books by LS, LLC.

ISBN: 9798884009264

This book is a work of fiction. Any similarities to real people, living or dead, is purely coincidental. All characters and events in this work are figments of the author's imagination.

Books by Lisa Suzanne

VEGAS HEAT: THE EXPANSION TEAM
Curveball (Book One)
Fastball (Book Two)
Flyball (Book Three)
Groundball (Book Four)
Hardball (Book Five)

VEGAS ACES
Home Game (Book One)
Long Game (Book Two)
Fair Game (Book Three)
Waiting Game (Book Four)
End Game (Book Five)

VEGAS ACES: THE QUARTERBACK
Traded (Book One)
Tackled (Book Two)
Timeout (Book Three)
Turnover (Book Four)
Touchdown (Book Five)

VEGAS ACES: THE TIGHT END
Tight Spot (Book One)
Tight Hold (Book Two)
Tight Fit (Book Three)
Tight Laced (Book Four)
Tight End (Book Five)

VEGAS ACES: THE WIDE RECEIVER
Rookie Mistake (Book One)
Hidden Mistake (Book Two)
Honest Mistake (Book Three)
No Mistake (Book Four)
Favorite Mistake (Book Five)

Visit Lisa on Amazon for more titles

Dedication

To my favorite three.

Chapter 1
Danny

I sit on the balcony of my second story room as I stare out over the ocean.

Is this what heartbreak feels like?

I'm not sure since I've never dealt with this kind of thing before, but my chest is heavy with a constant, dull ache. I'm tired since I didn't sleep all night, and my head hurts—also for the same reason, probably, unless it's because of the heartache. My stomach is in knots, and I have no idea how to cope with all this.

I shouldn't be heartbroken. She made promises to me. She loves *me*. But all the same…

She's marrying someone else today.

I should order lunch.

I never ate breakfast.

I can't eat.

I think about calling room service for a drink, but that would require me to get up.

I can't get up.

I glance at my phone again. It's cemented into my palm, ringer volume at full blast, and still…nothing.

She hasn't called.

She hasn't texted.

Maybe she actually wanted Brooks after all.

Maybe I've just been a fucking idiot believing in the lies, believing that she wanted me too. Maybe I was the other man this whole time, and she played me for a fool.

Those thoughts sneak their way in, but I know the truth.

She loves me. She loves me the same way I love her. It's devotion and adoration. It's pure and simple. It's everything.

And yet, she's marrying someone else today.

It doesn't spell the end for us, which is something I never thought I'd say given my painful past regarding infidelity and my very strong beliefs when it comes to cheating.

But I still had this little glimmer of hope somewhere deep down that she believed enough in *us* to end this sham and choose me.

I gave her my blessing to go through with it. I told her to do it. I shouldn't have. I should have fought harder. I should have begged her to stay. I should have done *something*, anything.

So I sent bacon.

What the fuck more could I have done?

The answer is lost on me.

I thought bacon and donuts might've gotten through to her.

I guess I was wrong—about a lot of things. Not just the bacon.

And that hurts more than it should.

I've been right here for most of the day, waiting to hear from her as a pit of despair knots my stomach.

I can guess *why* I haven't heard from her—not that it makes things any better. I'm certain her father is hovering over her. Maybe he even took her phone. Maybe he saw my message.

Maybe he never showed it to her. Maybe he deleted it and she doesn't know I'm thinking about her—only her, nonstop as anxiety plagues me that she's marrying the wrong man.

I could go stop it.

I could fight my way in somehow.

But I also know security is tight. It should be, after all. One of the biggest stars in the world is getting married, and she needs her protection.

And meanwhile, the bride who always is a vision of beauty is being primped and primed for her wedding day as she prepares to marry the wrong man.

My phone rings, vibrating in my hand as my heart lifts with hope, but it's only Rush calling.

I send it to voicemail.

He knows today's Alexis's wedding day. I'm sure the coverage is all over the place. I haven't brought myself to look yet.

I can't imagine seeing her in a wedding dress as she walks toward the wrong man.

My phone dings with a text, and I hurry to check if it's from her. It's not.

I scratch at the beard that I've grown over the last week. I haven't been in the mood for facial grooming, exactly, and every time I let it go for more than a couple of days, my face itches like hell.

At least it's a feeling. At least it's not numbness. That's what I keep telling myself.

Maybe I'll get used to it.

Rush: *Are you okay, man? Your sister is worried.*

The text is evidence enough he's worried, too.

My sister tries calling, too, and I wonder how long they talked about which one of them should call me first and how they decided on Rush instead of Anna.

I can't find it in me to reply.

Cooper calls, too. I don't answer.

My mom calls, and I nearly answer her call, but I don't.

Instead, I keep staring out over the ocean.

You know who doesn't call?

That's right.

Caroline Alexis Bodega.

It feels good to know I have a network of people who care about me, but that's little solace right now as I think about what our future will look like.

Can I really wait around until she's untied from him?

I hope I can. I told her I will. I want to be able to.

But I'm not sure.

What if it's more than a year? What if it's forever?

What if I end up alone when I had her right there, when we were so goddamn close we could taste it?

There's a knock at my door, and I lift to my feet. Is it her?

I race through my suite, look through the peephole, and sigh as I open the door. "Can I help you?"

"Sorry to bother you, sir," a maintenance man says. "We had a work request about a lightbulb. We can come back later."

"It's fine," I say, opening the door wider, and I move to return to my chair on the balcony.

Before I get outside, though, the man says, "Congrats on your win."

Do I look like I'm in the mood for conversation? "Thanks, man."

He nods. "I've been a fan of yours since your days on the Rockies. Helluva ballplayer."

"I appreciate that," I say, heading out to the balcony.

"My kid is a big fan, too," he hints.

I draw in a long breath through my nose and exhale through my mouth. I don't want to be rude, but I also don't want to be doing this. I'm not here to sign shit for this man. He didn't ask, probably because he's not allowed to, but I get where he's going.

I grab the room service menu and the pen on the nightstand. "What's your kid's name?"

"Maddox," he says.

To Maddox. Your dad got this for you. -Danny Brewer

My signature is illegible, but it's legit.

I hand the menu over to Maddox's dad. "Have a good day," I say, and then I escape to the patio, my phone still clutched in my palm as I wait.

Chapter 2
Alexis

I press my lips together and nod, but I'm not nodding at Gregory.

I'm nodding because I've made a choice.

Left to Brooks or right to Danny?

It doesn't escape me that Danny is to the *right*...as in the *right* choice.

My eyes meet Gregory's. "I need your keys."

His brows crease together. "You...what?"

"Give me your keys." My voice is a firm command representative of the strong woman I've turned into over the last twenty-eight years. I hold out my hand and set my other hand on my hip as I wait.

"Do you know what you're doing?" he asks quietly.

"Yes. I'm positive this is the right thing."

He nods once, and he pulls the keys out of his pocket. "I know he'll take care of you, Alexis."

I know he will, too.

"I'm in the first spot by the door. You should be able to sneak out without being seen." He pulls off his tuxedo jacket. "Wear this. It'll cover the dress from the shoulders down so nobody suspects anything."

I shrug into the jacket. "I have a Christmas Eve performance in Los Angeles I have to be at," I say quietly. "I will be back for that. I'll leave your car at the Ritz in Santa Barbara. Keys will be at the front desk. Give me a head start."

"Of course. I'll stall. Is an hour enough time?"

I nod, and I lean forward and wrap my arms around the man who has become so much more than a security guard and driver to me.

He's like a second father.

He's one of the only people I trust in the entire world…more so than my *actual* father.

"I love you, Gregory," I whisper on a quiet sob, and he squeezes me back.

"And you, Alexis," he says.

"Do you have Danny's mom's number?" I brush away some tears as I pull back from his embrace.

He nods.

"We'll be in touch with her," I say. "I'll leave my phone in the car so I can't be traced."

"I don't think that's a good—" he starts, but he stops short when he sees the death stare I'm giving him. "Of course, ma'am. Take care of yourself."

I reach out and squeeze his hand. I want to make sure he knows this isn't permanent. I know I have responsibilities to come back to. Filming will resume in a couple of weeks, and I'm not missing my chance at the Academy Award, and I will continue to need Gregory in my life.

I slip off my *engagement ring* that never meant anything to me and place it in Gregory's palm. I tighten his hand over it and squeeze his hand one last time.

"Don't you forget that *I* am the one who hired you, Gregory," I say. "Not my father. I just need the next nine days, okay? Tell my dad you left the keys in my bridal suite, and I snuck out the bathroom window and stole the car."

He nods, and I give him one long last look before I grab my purse and bolt the hell out of there, white wedding dress and all.

I see security guards in the parking lot—extras hired to make sure nobody can get in.

But they didn't say anything about people getting *out*.

I should have grabbed some clothes or something since all I have on me now is my wedding gown, but I was just thinking about how I needed to get out. I figured I'd take the rest as it came.

I find the Yukon exactly where Gregory said it would be. I look left and right before I run to it, and I start the ginormous SUV.

I glance out of the windshield and spot the helicopters circling, the paparazzi doing anything they can to steal the first peek of my big day.

Fuck that.

Even *they* don't deserve the complete and utter lie this wedding is.

I peel out of the parking lot, determined to make this right.

Determined to make *my life* right again.

It takes me a minute to get used to this thing. It's about four times the size of my little white Audi, and it's been probably two years since I've even driven *that*. How the hell does Gregory ease in and out of traffic so easily the way he does?

I get to the main road and merge onto it, getting as far away as fast as I can. I know Gregory said he'd stall, but we need to move.

I use the digital assistant function on my phone to ask for directions to the Ritz in Santa Barbara, and the map magically appears on the audio interface in front of me.

And then I cruise.

I'm probably speeding.

I don't care.

I'm in a race against the clock. I'm in a race for my life.

The car estimates it'll be twenty-three minutes until I arrive, and I push the gas pedal a little harder, hoping to gain a little more space between my dad and whatever comes next.

I know he will search for me. He will do everything he can to find me.

But *I* will do everything I can to stay hidden.

Thoughts start to creep in on me about what I'm leaving behind.

Did I make the right choice?

I'll know when I show up at his room, I guess.

Will Gregory be okay?

He will be. Just as I assured him that I am the one who hired him, I know he'll be waiting for me when I return. But I also know my father. He won't be happy that Gregory let me get away.

I don't want him to bear the brunt of my father's wrath, but at the same time…he's protecting me even if he's not with me. And he's damn good at his job.

My mind wanders to what's happening at the wedding.

Are the guests gathered there waiting for the bride to walk down the aisle? What are they thinking as the wait that should have been a couple minutes is stretching into more?

Bases Loaded

I wonder what's going through my dad's head right now. Has he realized I'm gone yet? Likely not, since Gregory said he'll stall.

I wonder what Brooks thinks. I wonder if Brooks will even care if I don't show or if he was just along for the ride the way I was.

I wonder what Gregory is doing right now. I picture him walking up the aisle solo and the guests looking around as they start to realize that something is wrong. I imagine the look on my dad's face, the set jaw, and the angry, cold eyes as Gregory delivers the news that I'm gone and so is his car. I don't think he will deliver that news quite yet. I wonder if he crafted a story about how I've locked myself in the bathroom and won't come out, and then they'll break open the door and find the window open because Gregory is smart enough to cover all the bases.

And maybe worst of all, I wonder what my dad will say when I finally return home.

Because as much as I want this to be forever, I know it can't be.

I have responsibilities to return to. I can't stay on the run forever.

Nine days. We have nine days.

But right now, as I lower the driver's side window and let the California breeze whip my hair around, I've never felt more free in the last twelve years—and maybe in my entire life.

Chapter 3
Danny

The maintenance guy leaves, and I'm left in the silence of the ocean gently rolling against the shore once more.

I stare at the water, hoping for peace and tranquility, but my roaring mind and rolling stomach have other plans.

When there's another knock at my door, I'm slower to get up this time.

Another fucking lightbulb? Another fucking signature? I want to yell it at the maintenance man.

I don't bother with the peephole this time, instead angrily throwing the door open, poised to give this dude a piece of my mind when all I want is a little alone time.

But it's not the maintenance man at all.

My jaw drops as I stare at the woman standing in front of me.

She's wearing an oversized man's tuxedo jacket, but the unmistakable white silk billowing underneath it is a clue that she just came from her wedding.

Her hair is curled in gorgeous waves, a pearl clip pulling some of it back out of her face, and her skin is flawless. *She* is flawless.

It takes me a few seconds to realize she's actually here.

She's actually here.

"Run away with me," she begs, her beautiful voice that's always a song carrying over to me and melting every last fear, every last anxiety, every last nerve clear away to make room for the overwhelming love coursing through me.

"Always," I say, pulling her into my arms and my room. I let the door close behind her as I yank her against me, and I stare at her a beat, trying to reconcile whether or not this is real.

She tips her chin toward me, and then my mouth crashes down to hers.

Oh, this is *definitely* real.

This kiss is messy and complicated, sort of like us. It's urgent and needy.

And it's so full of love that my chest feels like it could burst open.

I kiss her with everything I have, my mouth opening to hers as my tongue thrashes wildly, and she meets me step for step through the brutal force of need and lust and adoration coming together in this one kiss. Teeth clash together, and tongues batter, and I just want to carry her over to the bed and make love to her until neither of us can see straight.

She pulls back first, though, and the move dashes a bit of my hopes.

"We have to get out of here," she cries.

"What? Why?" I don't let her out of my arms. Now that I think about it, I might never let her go again.

She reaches up and strokes the beard that's grown in. "They'll be on their way soon. Gregory thought he could buy me an hour, maybe."

"Wait...what?" I ask, the fog of her words not really hitting me yet. "Why would Gregory need to buy you an hour?"

"Because I ran out on my wedding. I ran to you. I want to *be* with you."

"And only Gregory knows?" I ask, trying to get all the information.

She nods. "But my dad can track my phone, and I have no idea how much of a head start we have. I left it in Gregory's car, and we can leave the keys at the front desk, but I ran right to the room number you gave me when I got here, and surely by now they've figured out I'm gone and—"

I cut her off with another press of my lips to hers. "And they won't find us until we're ready to be found."

I let her go, and I run to my suitcase. I didn't bring many clothes with me, but this will have to do. I grab her a t-shirt and a pair of my shorts. "Here, put these on until we can stop somewhere and get you some clothes."

"I need help getting out of the dress," she says as she shakes off the jacket she's wearing.

"Who's is that?" I ask.

She clears her throat. "Gregory's. He thought it would disguise me long enough to escape."

Gratitude fills my chest. "Thank God for him."

"I do. Every day." She gets the jacket off, and I stare at her, my heart beating out of my chest.

"Jesus, Lex. You look..." I try to find the word, but none seem to fit what I'm really thinking.

"I look...?" she asks.

I clear my throat. "Like the woman I'm going to marry."

Her eyes mist over at that as she tilts her head and places a hand over her chest. She sings my name quietly, and I take a step toward her.

"Here, let me help you out of this."

She spins around, and I see the row of complicated buttons in the back.

"Fuck. How does this work?"

"Same way you eat an elephant. One bite at a time. Or, in this case, one button at a time," she says. I start the lengthy process, my fingers fumbling along the way. "Fuck it," she mutters. "Just rip the damn thing. It's not like I plan to *ever* wear it again."

"You got it." I yank at the buttons, and a few go flying off in different directions.

She laughs, and it's unbridled and full of joy.

I want to hear more of it.

I can tell she's nervous because of what she left behind. Her father will be looking for her soon. She's right…we need to get out of here.

She slips off the dress, and I can't help but stare at her body. I can't help but stare at *her*.

She pulls my t-shirt over her head. It's like a dress on her, but it's somehow perfect. "Vegas Heat," she says, fingering the logo a little. "My favorite team."

I offer a half smile. "Now covering my favorite body."

She grins, and she pulls on my shorts, pulling the strings hard and tying them tightly so they don't fall off of her. We need to get clothes for her stat.

But we can worry about it in the next town. Or, fuck, the next state.

We just need to get on the move as soon as humanly possible.

"What do you want to do with the dress?" I ask as I throw all my belongings into my suitcase.

"Pitch it?" she suggests. "Or we can leave it in the Yukon so there's no question about the fact that I was here."

I nod. "I can go put it in there if you'd like. Oh, and here." I toss her the Vegas Heat ballcap, and she slips it onto her head. "That hat has never looked better."

She's smiling again, and seeing her decked out in my gear is blindingly beautiful.

Or maybe it's just blindingly beautiful that she's here.

Either way, I finally feel that sense of peace I've been looking for since I checked into this beautiful place.

I finally feel like the future starts right the fuck now.

Chapter 4
Alexis

I wait in the room while he runs my dress down to Gregory's car. He said he will text Gregory from my phone that I'm safe and that the keys to the Yukon will be at the hotel desk.

I had to tell him where I hid my phone—under the backseat. I told him to leave it there.

He drops his suitcase at his rental car, too, and then he swings back up to the room to get me.

"We need to go," he says as he walks into the room breathlessly.

I lift to a stand from my place on the bed. I was hoping we had enough time to, you know...seal the deal.

"Why?" I ask.

"There was a text from Gregory that they're on their way here."

"Already?" My eyes widen. "What did it say?"

"Here," he says, handing me his phone. I look at the picture he took of my phone.

Gregory: *Alexis, where have you gone?*

Gregory: *We've tracked you to the Ritz Carlton in Santa Barbara. We're coming to get you.*

Dad: *How could you do this to me?*

These messages were sent nearly fifteen minutes ago.

Most certainly they're racing to get here.

Danny's right.

We need to go.

Now.

We race down to the parking lot, but it's an awfully long walk from his ocean view room to the parking lot on the other side of the hotel.

I wear his sunglasses and hat to protect my identity as best I can. With the huge shirt and shorts, nobody would ever look at me and think *oh hey, there's Alexis Bodega*.

We get to the parking lot and spot another Yukon pulled behind the one I parked half an hour ago. They're already here.

I thought Gregory was buying me an hour.

My dad wasn't selling that much time, apparently.

Nobody is near the car, and we both look around, shrug, and start to make our way toward the lot to get into Danny's rental.

But we both stop short when we spot my father walking out from the front lobby with Brooks and Gregory trailing behind him.

My dad looks furious. Brooks doesn't look quite as forlorn and sad as a man who was just left at the altar should look. And Gregory…well, he looks the same. Blank expression as he surveys the area.

The party of three heads toward the two Yukons, and we duck behind a row of hedges.

Bases Loaded

We watch my dad open the front driver's side door and look around, obviously searching for something, and I'm guessing it's my phone—which Danny says he hid even better than I did. And even if he manages to find and unlock it, it won't matter. He won't find what he's looking for. I was smart enough to delete Danny's contact from my phone before I hid it in Gregory's car.

"God dammit!" I hear my father yell even from here.

"Where's your car?" I whisper.

He nods to the first row of cars. I parked in the first row, too, but on the opposite side of where we're standing.

"I could sneak over to my car and pull around to the driveway back here to pick you up," he suggests, nodding toward the side of the building where we'll be out of sight.

I nod. "Let's do it."

He leans down to drop a kiss to my lips, and his eyes catch mine before he takes off. His hold a gleam to them that makes my pulse race a little faster. "Adventure awaits." He wiggles his brows before he grabs the hat off my head and pulls it down low over his eyes.

I can't help a little laugh at the sentiment. I feel like I'm in some suspense movie where I'm hiding out from the people trying to find me.

Instead…it's not a movie. It's my actual life.

And I will play the hell out of this part if it means Danny is on the other side.

Danny walks casually toward his car like any other man walking toward a car in a parking lot. He does nothing to raise suspicion, and my father makes one fatal mistake.

He puts his trust in Gregory to keep watch.

I see Gregory as his eyes connect with Danny, but Danny keeps his head down low. Gregory turns toward my dad and says something, and for a second, my heart fills with fear.

I should know better.

I should know I can trust Gregory to help orchestrate our escape.

But they got here awfully fast.

Given how everyone else in my life has betrayed my trust, why shouldn't I believe he will, too?

I just want to run away for a little while. I just want to be with Danny. I just want to escape my life and the utter circus it has become.

My dad bends down further into the car and searches under the seats. It'll be mere seconds before he finds the phone, and Danny reaches his car just in time. He fires it up, casually backs out of the space, and pulls onto the main road.

Wait a second...

Is he leaving me here?

My heart palpitates loudly in my chest as I watch everything unfold, and then I watch as Danny turns into the next entrance of the hotel and pulls up along the driveway behind me. I glance over at my dad, who obviously located my phone since he's now looking at it, and Gregory manages to turn him so he's facing away from us.

I run to the car and leap inside, my heart racing wildly, and Danny exits the parking lot. I turn around to see if my dad or Brooks is watching us, but they're totally oblivious to the fact that the person they're looking for just managed a clean getaway.

My heart isn't quite calm yet, though. We may have made our first escape, but that doesn't mean they'll stop searching for us. My father is relentless and will stop at nothing to find me.

Which is why we need to find a damn good hiding spot.

Chapter 5
Alexis

He merges onto the highway and heads north, which is probably the smartest plan since my father will think I'm going south—back home to Los Angeles.

I have no real destination in mind, and I'm not sure if Danny does, either.

"Where are we going?" I ask.

"Who cares?" He reaches over to squeeze my hand. "We're together. That's all that matters to me."

I draw in a deep breath and exhale, and it feels like I'm breathing in some happy form of freedom and exhaling the oppression I've lived under for the last twenty-eight years.

It sounds dramatic since I have a good life. But the good life has come at the expense of nearly every personal relationship I have, including the one I have with my only surviving parent.

But I have Danny now. He's my family. He's my home.

"When do you have to be back?" he asks quietly.

"Christmas Eve." I sigh. "I'm doing a live special with a few other singers in Los Angeles. We've already practiced and pre-recorded some segments."

"And I assume Brooks and your dad will be there?"

I nod. "Most certainly."

"That gives us nine days," he says. "How hard do you want to run?"

My brows dip. "What do you mean?"

"I mean...do you want disguises? Clothes? Do you want to be gone all nine days? Do you want to go somewhere remote where nobody will find us?"

"I want to run like I'm racing a marathon for my life," I finally say. "With you. I want to walk in the sunshine down the street holding your hand without worrying someone will find us. I want to just be normal for nine days. Can we just be *normal* for nine days?"

He presses his lips together. "Absolutely, Lex. Absolutely."

"I feel like I've hardly spoken to you since you went back to Vegas last week," I say.

"You haven't," he grunts. "But I understand why. Your father...he's a powerful man, and you were stuck."

"I was. But then I realized it was time to take control of my life." It sounds so simple now, but the truth is I have no idea what sort of complex consequences I'm leaving in my wake.

"And that led you to me?" he guesses.

"When I looked into my heart, I only saw you there. I couldn't go through with something as big as a wedding when it wasn't to *you*."

"So you're saying that your answer to my proposition last week might have changed?" His tone is filled with hope.

"I think if you asked me again, my answer might be different," I admit.

"Then maybe I'll ask again."

My heart races.

I hope he does.

We keep heading north with no destination in mind, and it's romantic and dreamy as we travel together, leaving our cares behind us. Leaving our entire *lives* behind us.

We're an hour north of Santa Barbara when I ask, "What ever happened with your father?"

"I bought us some time," he says.

"How?"

He lifts a shoulder. "I told him if he didn't stop threatening us, I would have an investigator look into his secrets, too."

My brows dip. "But you already did that."

He nods. "I did. And ultimately, using his fatal illness against him felt wrong."

My heart seems to grow bigger at his words. He's taking the high road here even though his father isn't. "Even though he's using it against you? God, Danny. You're such a good man. Do you know that? What you're doing should be proof enough that you'll never be like him."

He grips the wheel a little tighter then glances over at me. "Before you shower me with compliments, you should know that I decided to have Chloe see what else she can find on him."

"I stand by what I said. You're a good man, and I'm so lucky I found you."

He leans over to bump my shoulder with his. "I'm the lucky one."

"Do you think he'll talk once he finds out we're both missing?" I ask.

He shrugs. "He's a total wild card, but Chloe is working hard to find what we need. I'm sure he'll be in touch before he does anything. He has to try to squeeze more money out of me first."

"Good point. I'm so sorry for what you're going through, Danny."

He huffs out a mirthless chuckle. "You're going through some shit of your own, babe. Good thing we have each other."

Good thing we have each other.

Truer words have never been spoken.

"Are you getting hungry?" he asks a half hour later. "San Luis Obispo is coming up and they should have plenty of options."

I nod. "I am. You?"

"I haven't eaten all day. My stomach was in knots," he admits, and my chest tightens.

"I'm so sorry for what I put you through." My voice is soft as I reach over and rest my hand on his thigh.

"I'm sorry for what you had to go through," he says, reaching down and squeezing my hand. He clears his throat. "We could get gas here, too, and if you want, we could stop somewhere and grab some clothes for you and whatever we need to disguise ourselves."

"Oh, good idea. I have literally nothing except my purse, which I thought to grab when I left. But I don't think I want to use anything in it anyway or my dad can trace my location."

"Good call. In fact, we should pay cash for everything. Both of us so we can't be traced," he says. "But I don't have any cash."

"Then let's get some while we're here. It'll take my dad some time to hire someone to trace your credit card anyway, and we'll be long gone from here by then."

He twists his lips as he glances over at me. "Are you having fun with this?" he asks.

I can't help a little laugh. "You know what? Abso-fucking-lutely."

"Did you just say *fuck*?" he demands.

"Indeed I did just say *fuck*," I confirm.

"God, I love you," he murmurs.

We pull into a gas station, and he fills up. And then we pull into a Target parking lot.

Bases Loaded

The last time I was in a Target, I was seventeen and relatively unknown.

And back then...it was one of the greatest stores I'd ever been in.

I pull the hat down low, and with his beard, he's relatively unrecognizable, but he keeps his head down as we walk in.

"Grab a cart," I say. "We're gonna need some essentials."

As it turns out, essentials are a completely new wardrobe, a couple of suitcases for easier travel, all kinds of make-up and toiletries, and, naturally, road trip snacks including donuts. Danny grabs some things, too, and we head toward the checkout, where our bill totals over nine hundred dollars.

Yep. Still one of the greatest stores I've ever been in.

Chapter 6
Danny

One trip to Target plus some chicken from El Pollo Loco, and we're ready to disguise ourselves for the next nine days.

I've never had so much fun at a Target before.

But I've also never gone to one with Alexis, and I've never been to one when I was on the run from the father and would-be husband of the woman I love.

What a fucked up situation.

Alexis makes everything more fun, and she also makes everything an adventure—and this adventure is one I definitely wasn't expecting when I got out of bed this morning.

But here we are, on the run for the next nine days, and I don't know if I've ever seen her more joyful. I don't know if *I* have ever been more joyful, either.

This is all really working for me.

We've never had this much time together. We got lucky in the house when we filmed that commercial, but never nine whole days of unlimited time together.

Never nine whole days where we aren't both booked up with tons of other obligations.

I don't know if this will ever happen again, either. Between my long season and her tours and movies, we lucked out that the wedding was set to take place right before the holidays when everything seems to shut down.

I'll take it.

It feels like a long time stretching out before us, but I know it'll be over before I even blink my eyes.

I don't want it to be over.

I want to find a way to stretch this into forever.

I check the map as I eat my chicken and see a place about two and a half hours up the road that I've always heard great things about as an idea forms in my head. We could go there. We could stay in a house where nobody will see us.

We can spend the next nine days naked if we want.

And I definitely want to…but I also want to do a few other things with her.

And we don't have to limit ourselves to staying inside. We could disguise ourselves and go out. Tour the town. Live life. Be normal—just like she wants.

I'll need my mom's help, though. Not with the naked part. I've got that under control. But with booking a place and some of the other details…we may need some help there.

And so once we're back on the highway, I say, "I have an idea of somewhere we can go, but I think we'll need my mom's help to pull it off."

"Let's do it," she says. "Give her a call. I can't wait to talk to her."

The thought that they're already close warms my heart.

Bases Loaded

I dial her up on the car system, and we both hear her voice through the Bluetooth a minute later.

"Danny!" she answers cheerfully. "Thank God you called me back. I've been so worried about you!"

I roll my eyes, and Alexis chuckles softly.

"Well, I have some news," I say. "And I'm not alone."

"You're not alone?"

"Hi Tracy," Alexis says.

"Oh!" my mom squeaks. "Alexis, honey. Are you okay?"

"I've never been better," she says, and she catches my eye.

I grin.

"What happened?" my mom asks, and I realize I haven't actually heard the entire story yet myself. It's been sort of a whirlwind of a day.

"Well, all I could think about all morning was Danny, and I was just going through the motions. Hair, make-up, dress. None of it was what I wanted. But then I was in the bridal suite getting ready to walk down the aisle, and my dad came by. He said he was proud of me for doing the right thing, and maybe I'd even change my mind about Brooks. Something inside me snapped as I realized I was doing the right thing for *him*, and maybe for *Brooks*, but not for me. I haven't changed my mind about Brooks in the four years we've been pretending to be together, so I'm sure as hell not going to change my mind now."

"There's our girl," my mom breathes.

I reach over and rest my hand on her thigh as I accelerate down the highway. I want to just fucking get there even though I don't have an exact destination in mind yet.

"Danny had texted me where he was, and Gregory was supposed to help me get down the aisle," she continues. "He told me it was time, and I looked to the door where Brooks was waiting, and then I looked to the door that would give me my freedom. I didn't care about the consequences. I only cared about being with Danny. So I took Gregory's keys and ran."

"Oh, honey. That must have been so hard for you. Won't they be looking for you?" she asks.

"They already are. They tracked me to the hotel where Danny was, but we managed to dodge them before they caught us," she says.

"And now we're just driving," I finish.

"What can I do to help you two?" she asks, and it's exactly what I was hoping she'd ask.

"I had an idea for somewhere I wanted to land for the next few days, but we need your help booking a rental. I was thinking a Vrbo so we'd have privacy, but if I put it on my credit card, it'll be traceable."

"Consider it done," she says. "Where, how long, budget?"

"Carmel, on the beach with a big balcony and a view, single family home, tonight through…" I trail off and glance over at Alexis, who shrugs.

"Forever?"

I laugh. "Let's do five nights. If we have to bolt early, so be it. No budget."

"You got it," my mom says. "I'll text you the details when I have them, including the code to get in."

"Thanks, Mom. You're the best," I say.

"I love you. Both of you," she says. "You take care of yourselves and be safe. Call me if you need anything."

"Can you text Gregory to let him know we're safe but no other details?" Alexis asks.

"Of course, honey. Anything else?"

"Can you text me your credit card info so I can order some groceries?" I ask. "I'm sorry to even ask, and I promise I'll pay you back for everything."

"On it," she says.

We say our goodbyes and hang up, and Alexis breathes out a sigh of what seems to be relief.

"You okay?" I ask.

She nods. "Carmel is one place I've always wanted to visit, but I've never been to."

I look over at her with a smile. "In about two and a half hours, all that changes."

She nods, leans back against the headrest, closes her eyes, and she's never looked more relaxed or content to me in all the time I've known her.

Chapter 7
Alexis

We pull into the driveway of the address Danny's mom texted, and we're in for a real treat for the next few days as I looked up the house after she sent over the information. The place is gorgeous, with expansive ocean views on a rooftop deck with couches and lounge chairs.

When we arrive, the sun is just starting to set, which means we'll have gorgeous views as the water swallows up the sun.

We race up to the rooftop deck once Danny inputs the code into the keypad by the front door. We don't even give ourselves time to check out the gorgeous all white and bright décor of the place before we head right up, and he drags me against him as we look out at the sunset.

We can hear the gentle rolling of the waves from where we are. It's the same ocean and shoreline that Danny was looking out over when I arrived earlier today, but everything has changed now.

Everything.

I rest my head on his chest.

I should be concerned about what I left behind.

But in this moment, I'm not.

I'm where I'm supposed to be. I'm happy. Maybe for the first time in my life, I'm content.

But nine days will pass in a flash, and we'll return to Los Angeles for the Christmas Eve special.

The thought rumbles a bit of anxiety in the pit of my stomach, but I push it away for now.

Because right now, I want to enjoy the beautiful views in the arms of the only man who has ever loved me the way love is supposed to be.

We stand there wrapped in this sweet embrace until the sky turns dark, and then I hear his voice rumble up from his chest.

"We should order some food. Maybe move the car into the garage—it'll be safer in there."

I nod, and we head downstairs, flicking on lights and checking out our home away from home for the next few days. I've always loved California, but there's something special about this place.

"Do we have to order food?" I ask.

"Are you hungry?"

I nod. "Getting there."

"Then we should get something." He gives me a confused look.

"I mean…can we go out?"

The crease between his brows deepens. "You want to go out to dinner?"

I nod, and I move in closer to him. "I want you to take me on a dinner date somewhere normal, and then I want you to bring me back home and fuck me until I can't see straight."

He shifts and clears his throat. "Jesus. You have yourself a deal. Unless you want to reverse the order."

I grin. "I do, but I need to feed you first so you have more stamina."

"When it comes to you, I have plenty of stamina. But food first." He nods resolutely, and then he searches what's around us. "Pizza?"

I nod. "Perfect. But first, I need to change and probably disguise myself a little."

"I should, too. I'll pull the car into the garage and grab the bags from Target." He disappears for a few minutes while I check out all the rooms. The primary bedroom on the second floor is huge and gorgeous with its views overlooking the ocean, and I settle onto the bed and look outside while I wait.

And then I think twice. If he walks in and I'm on the bed, we'll never get pizza.

Not that I'd be complaining, but I really am starting to get hungry.

I head back downstairs and help him carry the bags in, and then I choose an outfit.

I look in the mirror.

I still look very much like Alexis Bodega.

I realize it's because I *am* Alexis Bodega, but it's not like I can just buy a box of hair dye and suddenly look different, given that my hair is already dark. I bought a box that claimed it could lighten hair up to three levels without any bleach, so we'll see if it does the trick. Tomorrow, maybe.

Tonight, I pull my hair up into a messy bun. The *real* Alexis Bodega would never be seen with a messy bun in public.

I put on heavy make-up to disguise my appearance. I'm not sure whether it'll work or not, but I give it a try.

I think about cutting bangs. That would do the trick.

But then I'll have bangs, and I'm not sure I want them. I'll be on television in nine days, and I still need to be…well, *me*. My brand.

Even if everything else around me is changing.

And even as I think it, I realize…I don't care about my brand anymore.

"Danny? Danny!" I yell.

He appears in the doorway to the bathroom a minute later. "Whoa. The goth look looks…hot on you."

I laugh. "Too much?"

"You don't look like Alexis Bodega," he says. "Carrie, maybe."

My chest warms at his words. "I need to cut my hair, and I need you to do it for me."

"Cut your…cut your…" he stutters.

"Hair. It's just hair. It'll grow back."

"It's up, though. Nobody will recognize you. And with the hat you bought at the store that isn't Vegas Heat, nobody will know. You don't have your entourage following you, Gregory is nowhere in sight, and I don't really look like me with this shit on my face, so even if somehow we've already been linked together, nobody will know."

I walk over and touch his beard. "I like this shit on your face," I say quietly. My eyes meet his, and his are dark blue and warm. "I want to feel it between my thighs later."

"Ugh," he groans. "Really? We're waiting until after dinner?"

"We're really waiting until after dinner," I say with a resolute nod.

"Fine. Then let's get a move on. I have thighs to tickle and a gorgeous cunt to lick for dessert."

My eyes nearly bug out of my head as I clear my throat. "Uh, yeah…let's go eat."

We finally manage to get out the door, clothes intact, and I guess because I'm so used to having a security detail with me, I find myself looking around us even when we're in the car.

Bases Loaded

It feels like every car behind us is following us. At every stoplight, I think whoever is in the car next to us is staring into our car, recognizing who I am and ready to blast it to the media.

Maybe I'm just living in my own little world where I'm a bit delusional, overly cautious, and a touch egotistical, but the paranoia is real. Probably because I've been burned more than once before.

Maybe this wasn't such a good idea after all.

But I glance over at Danny and remember I'm not hitting up the pizza joint with some nerdy Brooks. I'm hitting up the pizza joint with a professional athlete who will protect me at all costs because he adores me to the ends of the Earth. I may not have Gregory with me, but I do have Danny, and I feel safe with him.

When we get to the parking lot and he pulls into a space, he glances over at me. "Are you sure you want to do this?"

I press my lips together and stare out the windshield as I consider how well he knows me. I probably shouldn't be surprised at this point, but I am. "Yes. It's all I want to do."

"Well, I knew it was important to you when it came before the sex."

I can't help a small laugh at that. His ability to make me feel comfortable even in this very strange situation in which we find ourselves is calming and a little terrifying at the same time.

It shouldn't be this hard to get out of a car and walk into a restaurant, yet I sit in the front seat, staring at the restaurant, wondering if this is the right thing to do. What if we get caught? What if my dad figures out where we are?

What if I have to go back home early and face reality?

"Let's go," I finally say. I open the door and get out of the car, the first step of what to anyone else would be a normal night out with their boyfriend, but to me, it's the first risk I'm taking at potentially being recognized.

But we weren't recognized at Target. Maybe we'll luck out again.

We step inside the restaurant, and it's dimly lit. Without my usual makeup and designer clothes on, I'm just another girl walking into a restaurant. And Danny's hat pulled down low paired with the Guns N' Roses tee he picked up at Target pairs well with my Mickey Mouse sweatshirt and jeans. We're a good match as he asks for a table for two. I keep my eyes down, glad I chose to wear the hat, too, and we're led to a booth.

The dim lighting bodes well for us, and we don't draw a whole lot of attention to ourselves other than the fact that we're a damn good-looking couple.

The booth keeps us out of the spotlight, and I order a glass of wine to calm my nerves. The waitress doesn't appear to recognize me. In fact, she barely even looks in my direction, instead focusing on Danny. I'm sure she's waiting for the end of the meal when he'll present his credit card so she can check his name, but we'll be paying cash to keep our tail clean.

We order our food and talk quietly across the table. The loud din of restaurant noise blocks our conversation from anyone around us.

"Is it everything you thought it would be?" he asks.

"I hope there's leftovers."

"Why?" I ask.

"I brought some gummies with me, so we might need a snack later."

I giggle. "Good thing we bought all those road trip snacks at Target, too."

"Oh, that reminds me." He pulls out his phone and asks if I want anything from the grocery store, and we place an order for pick-up after we're done eating here.

"By the way," I say before our pizza arrives, "I wish you would've told me about the gummies before we came here. It might've helped me relax a little."

"A little? You would've fallen asleep before we even walked in the door."

I grin. "You're probably right about that."

There's some commotion by the door, and I hear someone yell, "Oh my God, is it really her?"

I shrink back into the booth, keeping my eyes down as fear palpitates in my chest.

"It is! It's Maci Dane!" another voice yells, naming the popular singer married to the drummer of Vail.

The attention diverts toward her, and I'm glad another celebrity showed up. Nobody was paying attention to us to begin with, but now I feel even safer blending in with the crowd.

Our pizza arrives, and it's absolute perfection. Nobody gives us a second glance.

It isn't what I was expecting my dinner to be when I woke up this morning.

It isn't what my father expected my dinner to be, either. And which man sitting across from me is even more astonishing.

But this is about ten thousand times better than what was planned for me.

We pay in cash and head out.

For as big of a night as I built this up to be in my mind, it was simple. Easy.

Just like everything is with Danny.

It has been that way since we first met. The only complications are when other people interfere or our jobs get in the way. But things between us? Simple. That's what should have clued me in that it was always going to be the right thing.

"I think I might be too full for sex," I say.

Danny starts laughing. "Then we'll take a walk until you feel ready."

"Nah, I'll be okay."

I think about getting the party started right now by bending over the console, but I really am full, and we have the rest of the night—and the eight days that follow—to have as much sex as we want.

And I for one can't wait to enjoy every single second.

Chapter 8
Danny

The conveniences of this day and age are outstanding as we pull into the pickup area at a local grocery store. I figured I'd surprise her with bacon and donuts for breakfast and other essentials like whiskey and wine.

I pop open the trunk and the attendant tosses our bags in the back. "Thanks, Tracy," she says, and I nudge Alexis.

"Have a great night!" she says, pretending to be my mother who paid for our groceries.

I'm lucky to have my support system with my family, minus my father, of course, and I want to provide that same stability in Alexis's life. I'm beyond grateful for Gregory. Without him, she'd truly have nobody to trust in her circle—except for me.

And she will always have me. And now that we're in this beautifully scenic town and have all this time together, I'm going to ask the question again.

This time, I'm actually going to ask…not suggest. This time, I'm going to make it count.

And this time, she's going to say yes.

We make it home and put the groceries away, and then our eyes connect as we both know what time it is.

We have tonight plus four more nights here in this house. It's just the two of us, and clearly we can get away with going out to dinner. Maybe tomorrow I'll convince her to take a walk together in the sunshine.

It feels pretty damn good just to be normal.

But right now, I don't want to be normal. I want to be naked with my cock buried inside her.

"Are you ready to fuck me?" she asks casually.

"I've been ready since the last time I fucked you," I shoot back, and her eyes widen a little—the only outward sign that she's affected by my words. "Now get your ass upstairs and get naked on the bed. I'll be up shortly."

She raises her brows, and then she turns quickly and scampers up the stairs.

I decide to raid the kitchen for... *supplies* for our sex.

I grab a cup and fill it with ice cubes, and I take the bottle of wine, too, which I uncork while I'm down here. I think about grabbing some other supplies—olive oil, maybe, or some cookies. Whipped cream.

But I don't need any of that shit.

I also grab a kitchen towel to use as a blindfold.

I head upstairs, and much to my joy, I find her lying naked on the bed as requested.

My eyes heat as they fall onto her. How did I get so goddamn lucky? I set the cup and the bottle of wine on the nightstand then take the kitchen towel and hold it between my fingertips. "Close your eyes."

She gives me a curious glance and purses her lips, but she does it. I tie the towel over her eyes, making sure she can't see, and then I take one of the ice cubes out of the cup.

Bases Loaded

I start by running it along her collarbone and down to her nipple. It immediately hardens as she lets out an audible gasp.

I warm the other one with my lips as I keep moving the ice cube in circles around the tight bud, and then I switch sides, lavishing heat on the cold nipple with my mouth as I freeze the other side. It's hot and cold play, something we haven't done before, and it's sexy as hell listening to her sweet little gasps and moans.

I take my time with each nipple because time is finally on our side for once. I *love* her tits, and I could bury my face between them for the rest of the night.

My cock, however, has other plans.

It's begging for escape as it pulses painfully in my jeans. I don't know how much more of this I can take without giving it a stroke or two.

I force myself to hold it together as the ache intensifies. Once the ice cube is melted, I pick up the bottle of wine.

I splash a little onto her abdomen, and then I trail my lips down to lick it off. I trail my mouth back up to hers for a kiss, and she pulls back, still blindfolded.

"Pinot noir?" she guesses, and I chuckle.

I pull at her bottom lip and tip the bottle a little to give her a sip as a reward, and my lips are on her neck when she swallows.

I take a swig right from the bottle and set it on the nightstand again, and as fun as these props are, I'm ready to get to the main event. I kiss her again, our tongues tangling together with the cherry taste of the wine, and then I trail back down her body and toward her sweet, sweet cunt.

I tease her a little first, pushing her legs wider to give me more room. I kiss her hip, her inner thigh, and her pubic bone. I kiss the top of her pussy, and down each side, and then I find her clit with my tongue. I flick my tongue back and forth over it before I suck on it, and her hips jerk at the feel of my mouth.

"Oh God, yes, Danny," she murmurs, and her hands move into my hair as she holds my head down over her hot pussy. She writhes under me, and her sounds paired with her taste and her neediness nearly make me come.

I slip a finger inside her, and she's so fucking wet for me. So ready.

"Fuck," I groan. "You want me to fuck this cunt?"

"I want to suck your cock while you keep licking me," she says, shocking the hell out of me.

A sixty-nine with Alexis Bodega? Have I died and gone to heaven?

I shift off her and race to give the woman what she wants. I yank my jeans and boxers off, getting naked in record time, and then I turn around and slide into place, resting a knee on either side of her head. I fist my cock, stroking it a few times, before I slide it down between her parted lips.

Oh fuck.

The feel of her mouth is pure ecstasy, and I can't help but slide my hips down so she takes me all the way to the back of her throat.

That's right.

I'm fucking Alexis Bodega, America's sweetheart, pop princess who sings like a fucking canary, right in the mouth.

And it's glorious.

I lean forward and align my mouth with her pussy, using one elbow for balance while I use my other hand to part the lips of her pussy. I slide a finger in, and I lick her clit with rapid strokes. She moans, the sound humming on my cock in her mouth, and she brings a hand up to circle a vice-like ring around my cock while she keeps sucking on me. I slip out of her mouth to give her a second of recovery—or maybe it's to give *me* a beat before I'm about to jizz in her mouth—and then I'm right back at it.

I add another finger and twist them, curling up toward her G-spot, and she screams with my cock in her mouth. I can't help my grin as I keep fingering her, and I move my mouth to suck on her clit.

I shove my fingers in a little harder, and she starts to quiver. I've got her right where I want her. I flick my tongue across her clit a few times, and she falls apart. I don't drag my cock out of her mouth, but I do let up a little to let her fly through her release. As her pulses start to slow, I caress her pussy with my tongue, and then I pull back and start to really fuck her mouth.

She takes every last bit of me as I push into her mouth and pull back out, and she's greedy as she sucks on me, taking me like a pro.

It's not long before I lose it. Hell, I was about to lose it before we barely even started.

I'm about to pull out of her mouth to come, but she doesn't let me, wrapping her arms around my waist and holding me in place.

Jesus. Has there ever been anything hotter in the history of sex? I think not.

I come with a loud growl, and she sucks down every last drop of me, swallowing before I even pull out of her mouth. Once I do, she keeps her fist around me, stroking me a few more times.

I can't help a small laugh since my dick is so sensitive after that workout, and she lets go with a smile and a soft, breathless sigh.

It's the kind of sigh of contentment I want to hear from her every single day for the rest of our lives.

And I'm hoping today is the start of it.

Chapter 9
Danny

Eight days.

We have eight more days like this.

After the kind of night that lives purely in fantasies, we wake in each other's arms in the morning well after ten.

I don't get very many opportunities to sleep in. Being on tour means late nights and early mornings. It means restless nights in different hotels even though I have a custom tour bus. And filming also means late nights and early mornings.

But sleeping here in Danny's arms without having anywhere to be in the morning is a new experience, and it's one I want to relive over and over again.

Forever, if that's at all possible.

I don't move even when I wake. The curtains on the windows are closed, and part of me wants to get up and see the view in the morning, but the other part of me wants to spend forever right here.

I hear a soft sigh behind me.

"You're awake," he says quietly.

I twist in his arms to face him, and he's so handsome in the dim light coming in through the sides of the curtains. "I am. And so are you."

"I am."

"You been awake long?" I ask.

"A half hour maybe. I didn't want to wake you. You were so peaceful. Maybe even snoring a little."

I giggle. "I do *not* snore."

"Have you ever heard yourself sleeping?"

"Don't give me a complex," I mutter, and he chuckles.

"Fine. You don't snore."

"Told you."

"Bacon?" he asks.

"If we have to get up."

"We don't have to, but I'm hungry, and that bacon is calling my name. And the long johns."

"Bacon, long johns, and coffee on the roof?" I suggest.

He raises his brows. "Coffee?"

"I feel like I need extra fuel after the night we had," I admit.

"Then coffee, bacon, and donuts coming right up for my lady."

I just hope I still fit into the Christmas Eve dress that was selected for me months ago when I get back to LA.

We force ourselves to start our day, and twenty short minutes later, we're sitting on the rooftop deck at a little bistro table with two chairs, enjoying our breakfast. It's a beautiful, if somewhat chilly, day here in northern California, the high only sixty-seven, but Danny was sweet enough to bring a blanket up for me to wrap around my shoulders. Meanwhile, he's in shorts and a t-shirt.

Bases Loaded

He's not wrong. Everything about today is pretty damn perfect.

Just as I shove a huge bite of donut into my mouth, he asks, "Should we do something today? Maybe…I don't know. Take a walk on the beach or something?"

"Sure, I'd love to. I've actually always wanted to visit Carmel-by-the-sea Village," I say. "I've heard lovely things about the galleries and shops there, and maybe we can grab lunch."

He raises his brows. "Look at you getting all adventurous on me."

I laugh and lift a shoulder. "Last night gave me the confidence that we can do this. Are we risking it? Absolutely. But Maci Dane showed up to divert attention. I've heard this is a popular celebrity hangout, so I'm not even sure it would matter if we *were* recognized. And wasn't Clint Eastwood the mayor?"

"Where was this can-do attitude last night?"

"I needed you to fuck it out of me, I guess."

He laughs. "Plenty of more fucking available to help adjust your attitude any time it's needed."

"Thanks for that," I say, and I offer him a wink. "Actually, my attitude is starting to go south. Maybe after bacon you can fix that up for me?"

"Happy to oblige, ma'am." He nods cordially at me, and I sigh with contentment.

Bacon, the beach, and Brewer. Life doesn't get much better than this.

True to his word, he bends me over the bed and fucks me until I see stars after breakfast, and then we get dressed and put on our disguises. He still hasn't shaved, and I'm actually loving the bearded look. He always sports a bit of a beard, but this is bushier than normal and it was hot as hell between my legs last night.

I think I even got a tiny bit of rugburn—a wound I wear proudly.

We each put on our hats, and I cover up in my baggy Mickey sweatshirt and jeans.

We head out toward the shops, and with sunglasses, hats, and baggy clothes, nobody even gives us a second glance. In fact, we're *so* ignored it's almost a little insulting—not because I'm so used to the attention, but because I'm still a paying customer, but some of the gallery attendants look at us like we don't have a dime to spare on their precious artwork.

If they only knew the truth.

I own a private jet.

He's got one of the largest contracts a first baseman has ever had.

I think we're doing okay for ourselves.

We wander through art galleries and jewelry shops. We stop for lunch at a cute little bistro with a view. We don't buy anything other than lunch, and there's nothing big planned for the day. We're literally just walking down the street in the sunshine hand-in-hand like every other couple walking down the street here, and it's so…normal. And it feels so, *so* right.

We get to just be *us*, and it makes me realize how much private jets and baseball contracts and *money* are meaningless. What matters is love. Us. Being together. Falling more and more in love—madly. Deeply.

Finding the one person you can't see your life without.

And when I look into the future, I see Danny.

I see a baby with his blue eyes and my dark hair…maybe two or three of them.

I see a home that we share.

I see mornings like the one we shared today, and afternoons like this, where we're clutching hands as we wander down the street.

I just hope I'm actually seeing the future, and it isn't some faraway dream.

Because right now, it truly does feel like I'm living in a dream, and the way I'm feeling right now, I know we have no choice but to figure out how to make this last forever.

Chapter 10
Danny

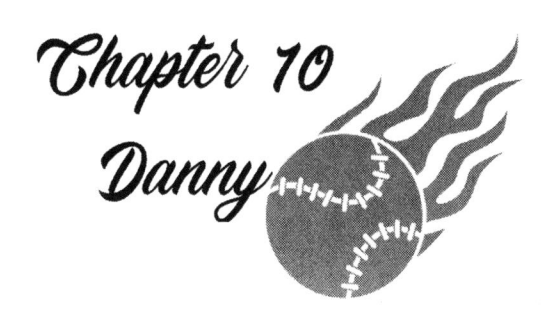

I waited until she needed to use the restroom while we were walking around the shops, and then I snuck back into the jewelry store.

It's not what I wanted to get her, but on limited cash and resources, it'll have to do. And the more I think about it, the more I can't help but think this *is* what I want to get for her...for *us*.

It's simple, just like today was. It's a vivid reminder that when it really comes down to it, this love we have is all that matters. Not money. Not other people's opinions. Not what other people want from us. Not big, fancy diamonds.

Could I spend half a million dollars on a bigger one?

Sure.

Do I need to?

No.

For what? Status? Fuck that.

The only status I care about is Alexis Bodega's marital one.

I have a game plan, and the pressure is huge. The bases are loaded, and it's the bottom of the ninth, and we're down by three with two outs. I'm up to bat.

It's a dream I've had since I was a kid—or maybe a nightmare, depending on what happens when the ball comes flying toward me at over ninety miles an hour.

I make a snap decision when I see it flying toward me, and tonight, I'm hoping for the grand slam.

When we arrive back home, we're both tired from a day out in the fresh air by the sea, but the box I ordered is waiting for us by the front door. She glances at me with concerned brows as she spots it at the same time I do.

"Did you order something?" she asks.

"I did."

"What is it?"

I lift a shoulder and raise my brows mysteriously. "Put on that black dress you got at Target," I say.

She raises a questioning brow at me. She's probably thinking how I'm asking her to put it on so I can do something nasty to her underneath it, and if she thinks that…well, she wouldn't be wrong.

But the other part of it is that I want to dress up for this.

I brought a suit with me in case she decided to invite me to the wedding, and I know the dress is the only dress she has with her.

I don't give her any hints as to what I'm thinking, and she goes up to the bedroom to change while I head up to the rooftop to unload the box and set up for my plan.

When I go back down to the bedroom to change my clothes, too, she's still getting ready. She's got the dress on, but she's fixing her hair and make-up in the bathroom with the door open.

She didn't need to fix a damn thing. She already looked perfect.

Bases Loaded

Everything is ready up on the rooftop. I just need to change, but I don't want her to see me until we're back upstairs, and I want to wait until the magical sunset hour.

I wait for her to finish getting ready, and when she emerges from the bathroom, I say, "We're having a date night in tonight. Meet me up on the rooftop deck at four-forty-five."

The sun sets early here in December, and I don't want to miss it. Sunset is just before five o'clock, and we'll be up there at just the right time.

It's a little early for the dinner I had planned, so we'll eat later. The food is up there keeping warm, the champagne has been poured, and the music plays softly in the background—all the things that were in the box waiting by the front door.

I thought about bacon and donuts and how to incorporate them into this moment. I thought about our time together and what we've been through, what would be meaningful and symbolic for us.

And ultimately I realized that what's most meaningful for us is the simplicity and ease with which we handle our relationship. People say relationships are hard work, but it's never *hard* with Alexis.

Well, my dick is. Always.

This thing between us is so effortless, so easy. The things that complicate it for us are always the outside forces trying to fight their way in.

But all we have to do is hold onto each other to fight all of them off.

And *that* is the root of the promise I plan to make to her today.

"I love these surprises from you," she says, and she walks over to gently kiss my lips before she disappears.

Get ready for a lifetime of them, I think to myself.

I think over my plan.

There are a million ways to propose to the love of your life. Publicly. Privately. In front of family. Naked—obviously not in front of family in that case. On a scoreboard or Jumbotron. Spur of the moment. Planned. Unplanned. On the beach. On a rooftop.

I didn't have a lot of time to plan this one, but we're in this place that feels pretty damn perfect, and we're alone—just as we have been for our entire courtship—and it just *feels* right.

That's what tells me it *is* right.

I rehearse the things I want to say while I get dressed.

I feel oddly calm, another thing telling me how right this is. It's like I already know her answer before I've even asked the question, and there's something comforting in that.

She always deserved better than the *marry me, not him* speech. She always deserved a better promise than *if you marry me, you won't have to marry him.*

And tonight…that's what she will get.

She will get all of me, something she's had since the moment we met, but something I will promise her now.

I glance at the clock, see I'm running out of time, and head upstairs.

I get down onto my knee, and then I wait.

Chapter 77
Alexis

I wasn't lying when I said I love surprises from Danny.

I love *everything* about Danny. He makes me happy. He makes me giddy. He makes me want to lay on my bed and kick my feet in the air with joy.

I've never felt this before in my life.

And waiting for four-forty-five is downright painful. I don't know what he has planned, but I know what I *hope* he has planned.

The last twenty-four hours have certainly been a whirlwind, but for the first time in my life, I'm making my own decisions.

And I've never been happier.

I stand in the kitchen with nothing to do other than stare at the clock. I glance out the window at the water. The sun is starting to lower down into it, and it's that beautiful time of day that's just peaceful and lovely.

I still worry we'll be found. I still worry we're taking too many risks.

But the risks are worth it, given where we've landed, and I've never felt safer than when I'm with Danny.

Gregory is amazing at making me feel safe, too, but this is something else entirely. Gregory watches out for my physical safety.

Danny covers physical, but he's also careful with my emotional safety. And I know that with my heart in his hands, I'll always be safe.

Eventually, the clock ticks to the time he said, and I head up to the rooftop.

When I get out there, it's lit with strings of lights and a full curtain of lights on the back side of the rooftop facing away from the ocean. Candles are lit and placed everywhere on the rooftop, and in the middle, surrounded by a glow of flickering flames, is Danny Brewer in a suit.

Let me repeat that. The baseball player is *in a suit*.

Have I ever mentioned that suits just *do it* for me?

The bad boy of baseball is all dressed up and he is hot as *hell*.

And he's down on one knee as he waits for me.

Tears heat behind my eyes as I walk slowly across the deck toward him. Once I'm standing in front of him, my pulse races as I reach down and take his hands in mine.

He looks at me confidently, and then he begins speaking from the heart.

"My best friend once asked me who my dream girl was, and even before I met you, it was you. Once I was lucky enough to meet you in person, that was only confirmed. You're smart, and you're talented, and you're beautiful, but over the last nine months, I've gotten to know your heart, too. You love bacon and donuts, and you love your music and your fans, and you love acting. But somehow, amidst all that, you also love *me*, and that is something I never saw coming. The things that are important to you are important to me, and that has become just being together. I want to be with you forever, Caroline Alexis Bodega. I want to wake up with you in my arms. I want to stroll through shops in disguises and laugh and hit up pizza joints together. I want to travel on tour with you, and I want you in the stands cheering me on. I want to support you in everything you want to accomplish in this life, and I want to hold your hand and cling to you while together we fight against the forces trying to push us apart. I love you, Lex. I didn't think love was in the cards for me, but all it took was meeting my dream girl. So today, I ask you to please make the final piece of my wildest dream come true by saying yes. Will you marry me?"

My heart very nearly bursts, and my chest tightens at his words. I've never heard anything so beautiful. I've never *seen* anything so beautiful as the man on his knee in front of me saying these wonderful words to me, asking me to marry him. Asking me to *be* with him.

Asking me. Not *telling* me.

Asking me to make a choice for what I want out of this life.

And that is the key to all of this.

He respects me enough to ask. He *loves* me enough to ask.

"Oh, Danny," I whisper. "I love you so, so much. Yes, I will marry you."

He rises to a stand and pulls me into his arms. His lips collide with mine as we seal our new engagement into a promise.

I would marry him right this second if I could.

I want to.

I want to be married to him when we return home to Los Angeles. I want to start building our life together. I want to buy a home and make it ours. I want to move out of my dad's house and start fresh. I want to make my own choices and be my own person instead of being the brand that's always been expected of me.

If I truly want younger girls to look up to me, then maybe this is the way. Choosing my own life. Making my own path. Being the authentic person I want to be rather than the woman I've been scripted to be.

And it all starts right here, right now.

He pulls back and reaches down into his pocket. When he opens his hand, he has two rings in it. One is a platinum man's ring, and the other is a simple, gorgeous eternity band made of diamonds. "I don't have an engagement ring, but I bought bands downtown today. I wanted to get you something you'd want, but I also wanted to—"

I shake my head as I cut him off. "I don't need an engagement ring, Danny. All I need is your love. Your promise. Your commitment."

"You have it all," he says, and his lips press to mine warmly again. He pulls back and leans his forehead down to mine. "Forever."

"You have it all from me, too. Forever."

His lips tip up in a smile. "I think we just wrote our vows."

"I think you're right. And I think we need a photo to commemorate this moment."

He slips his phone out of his pocket and pulls up the camera.

We both smile as he snaps the selfie, and he's about to take another one when I say, "I want to marry you before Christmas Eve. Before I have to get back to my life and everything I left behind."

He hits the button, and I can't wait to look back at the shock on his face later, captured forever in a photo.

"Are you sure?" he asks as he lowers the phone. His voice is soft and vulnerable.

I nod. "Positive. And before you get any crazy ideas as to why...well, I realized something today."

His brows draw together. "What?"

"That people spend their entire lives searching for what I found with you, and I don't want to waste another second of this life not being your wife."

His eyes heat a little at my words. "My wife," he echoes.

He draws me into him, crushing me against him. "Then let's get married."

"Let's get married," I murmur.

A part of me feels like I should be worried about rushing this. How are we ever going to plan a wedding in the next week?

And that's when I realize…simple.

I'll call his mom, and we'll drive down to San Diego, and we'll do it with her help. It'll just be the two of us, plus Tracy and Anna. Maybe Cooper or Rush, whoever he wants to invite. It'll be quiet and intimate.

It'll be everything my father never wanted for the wedding of The Alexis Bodega.

And it'll be perfect for us.

Chapter 12
Alexis

He still crushes me to him, and I'm holding on tight because I don't ever want to let go.

We can work out the details later.

For now, we celebrate.

We love.

We hold on.

We embrace, and we kiss, and we make love.

We start our future together.

Before all that, though, we toast. He pulls back and walks over to the table where two glasses of champagne wait. He hands one to me and holds the other.

"To our future," he says, and I touch my glass to his just as the sun dips all the way down into the water.

The moment in this setting is sweet and romantic, as is the champagne, and we each finish our glass while we hold hands and stare out over the water.

Once we're each holding an empty glass, he takes mine from my hand and sets it back down beside his, and then he takes me into his arms again.

He drops his head down as his lips find mine, and this kiss holds a sense of peace to it. It's not urgent and hurried because it no longer has to be. We're not limited even to the next eight days. We're only limited to the time we each have here on this earth.

His tongue is relaxed and smooth against mine as he holds me against him, but the way his hips shift to show me how he's ready for more tells a different story.

He wants to take his time, but I think somehow he can't with me.

We're trained to be fast, but tonight, I'm going to take it slow. And to that end, I decide to take the lead.

I grab his hand and pull him over to one of the lounge chairs, and I slide his suit jacket down his arms before I push him down onto it. He raises a brow, obviously liking this new side to me, a side that has never come out before and only is tonight because he's given me the confidence to explore it.

I settle on top of his lap, straddling his hips as I set a knee on either side of him, and he reaches around me to pull me close—topping from the bottom, but I wouldn't expect anything less from Danny Brewer. He tangles his fingers in my hair as he deepens our kiss, and I bring my palms up to cup his jaw, the longer hair there coarse between my fingertips and sexy as hell.

He trails his lips from mine down my neck and into my cleavage, and I grind my hips down against his. He moves his hands from my hair as his fingertips lightly roam my body, settling down on my hips as he pulls me down at the same time he pushes up. I pull his head more firmly into my chest, and he reaches up from my hips to dip into the top of my dress. He pulls one of my breasts out past my bra and over the low-cut neckline, and he sucks my nipple into his mouth. His tongue circles around and around until my nipple forms a tight bud, and then I feel the slight edge of teeth, pleasure mixing with pain at the feel.

He groans, and I shift over his hips again before I lean back off of him and reach down between us. I flick the button of his pants and pull the zipper down, and then I rub his cock over the outside of his slacks. I rub up and down, and he starts to move his hips to the motion of my hand.

He groans, and I take the opportunity to reach inside, gripping his shaft in my fist. I moan at how hard he is, at how *big* he is, at how much I want him inside me *right the fuck now*.

It's like I'm suddenly crazed with need, and I pull him out of his pants, shift upward, and use my other hand to move my panties to the side before I slide down on top of him, thankful for all the time I put into dancing for the strength in my legs to coordinate this all at one time.

My eyes find his, and I push down until he's all the way inside, heat pulsing between us as our eyes stay connected. I feel every inch of him as my body slowly takes him inside me, the friction intense as I sit all the way down on him. His take on a neediness—a need to move, maybe, or a need to fuck. A need to come. A need to have me and hold me forever.

And I'll satisfy as many of those needs as I can.

I feel him as he swells inside me, and then he shifts his hips down to force more friction. I rock on top of him, and he pushes up and pulls back over and over as we find the perfect rhythm together.

I grind down onto him as he arches up into me, his fingertips digging into my hips while I hold on tight around his neck. One of my nipples is still free from my dress, and it rubs against his chest, the fabric of his dress shirt rough against the sensitive skin.

I lean down when I start to feel my climax barreling down on me, and he arches up harder and harder with each drive. My lips find his, and this kiss is messier, needier as we both fight our way toward the climax.

And when it hits, it hits *hard*.

I can't help but yell out, and I'm sure people on the balconies and decks around us can hear us, but we're safe up here, safe with each other and safe together and safe from everyone else. And it's that feeling of protection and security here in his arms that helps propel me into a fierce and fiery orgasm.

I start to come, and I feel him as he lets go at the same time, swelling inside me as the jets of his come pulse into me over and over. My pussy takes it all, every last drop, as we each take what we need from the other one while giving what the other needs at the same time.

It's a beautiful moment unlike anything I've ever felt before, and I think part of the beauty is knowing this is the last man I will ever have sex with.

He's the only man I will ever love for the rest of my life.

And tonight is when all that begins.

Chapter 13
Danny

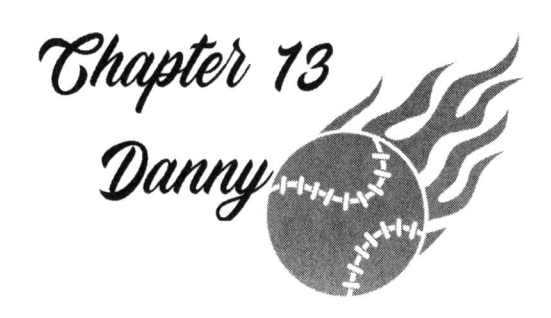

Well, I can officially confirm that engagement sex is the best sex.

I've had a lot of sex. I can't define what *a lot* is, but let's just say plenty.

And nothing holds a candle to what we just did up here on the roof.

It was intimate and powerful, sexy and beautiful. It was *different*.

I've never been engaged before. I've never fucked somebody I plan to call *wife* someday.

I've never been so goddamn crazy in love before, and all that combined together led us to this moment.

I hold her in the afterglow, and despite the strange road we took to get here, what we share overpowers everything else. It was inevitable that we'd end up right here—maybe not in this geographical location, but at this moment.

I don't care how we got here. I'm just glad to be part of the ride.

She shifts so I slip out of her, and there's a profound sense of loss once our bodies are physically separated. But emotionally, I still feel very much connected to her. And I always have, really—since the moment we started sharing those powerful types of feelings with each other.

And it's that connection that I think will help pull us through the times when we can't physically be together. It's that connection that bonds us together in a way that makes me feel confident that this is it for both of us. This is that once-in-a-lifetime type of love that I wasn't even searching for.

She shifts off me, and I tuck my cock back into my slacks and stand. I pull her into my arms, and we sway to the soft instrumental music playing in the background. I didn't know what music to play, so I YouTubed *romantic instrumental music* and started up the first playlist I found.

I'm starting to believe that she actually said yes.

It's starting to hit me.

We're really doing this.

And soon.

Eventually the call of hunger rings out, and I walk us over to the table. I pull her chair out and motion for her to sit, and then I serve up the plates that've been on warmers since we came up here.

I went with salmon and asparagus with a little fondue chocolate thing for dessert. It seemed romantic, but what the hell do I know about romance?

"This is so romantic," she says just as I have the thought.

Apparently I have more tricks in my arsenal than I knew.

"So you want to get married before Christmas Eve?" I ask, and the words should scare the hell out of me.

To my surprise, they don't. They feel as natural as breathing. She glances up at me as if to double check my reaction to my own words—as if to catch me feeling a little nervous about that, but I gaze back at her with the full conviction in us that I feel, and it seems to calm her.

She nods. "I do. And not because of my dad, or because of Brooks, or as some way to protect me from having to marry someone else. Because I want to marry you more than I've ever wanted anything in my life. Because when I'm with you, I feel like I can be who I really am in a way I've never had the luxury to be before. I don't have to play the part my father has carefully crafted for me, and being with you makes me feel…" She shakes her head a little as she thinks of the word and then lifts her shoulder. "Free."

"You *are* free with me, Lex," I murmur, and it tears at my heart that she's felt this way her entire life—and even more that she's felt this way but couldn't put words to it…until she met me. Until she caught a glimpse of everything she always deserved to have.

"I know I am." She tilts her head and brushes a tear away. "I want your mom there," she says suddenly. "And your sister. And whoever else you want to be there."

"What about on your side?" I ask.

"That *is* for my side. And in a perfect world, I'd want Gregory there, but I know that's not possible since we're on the run."

Maybe it is possible. *Anything* is possible, and I'm not really sure that's something I believed in until I met her.

"Where do you want to get married?" I ask.

She glances around. "This rooftop seems pretty perfect, but why don't we head down to San Diego and do it there? There's scenery all along the coast. We'll find our perfect rooftop deck in a place that's more convenient for your mom. And then we can go on our honeymoon to the place I always dreamed of going for my honeymoon."

My brows dip. "Where's that?"

"Disneyland."

"Disneyland?" I echo. Is she kidding right now?

Isn't Disney for kids?

The things I plan to do to her on a honeymoon—or any other time, really—are definitely not suitable for kids.

She nods. "Disneyland."

"All the tropical locations in the world, and you want to have your honeymoon with a mouse?"

She laughs. "You heard me right. Since I was seventeen, I haven't been able to walk around Disneyland without a crowd gathering around me. I want to dress up as Disney characters, wear a just-married sash, and get one of those buttons newlyweds get to wear. I want to spend the day feeling like a kid—riding rides, laughing, and eating Mickey ice cream bars. I want to be carefree and happy. And then I want you to take me back to our hotel room and treat me like the grown ass woman I am."

"Ass? Did you just say you want me to take your ass?" I raise a brow.

She shrugs. "I didn't not say it."

Oh, man.

I'm in for a lifetime of shocking words from this woman.

And I can't wait for every single second.

Chapter 14
Danny

We spend the night wrapped in each other's arms, and when morning dawns and we're both awake, we head up to the rooftop deck for bacon and eggs and start planning our wedding.

"We should get our license here in Carmel," she suggests. "That way if we're traced, it'll be to *here*, and it'll buy us time to head south to San Diego."

I tap my temple. "Smart thinking. Good thing I'm marrying you for your brain."

"I thought you were marrying me for my sexual prowess."

I shoot her a cheesy wink. "All part of the full package."

"I'd like to stop at a shop we were in yesterday, too. I saw a dress I liked and I can't stop thinking about it," she says. "And maybe dinner out again tonight. I don't really want to leave this place, but I know we have to."

"I don't, either," I murmur. I reach across the table and take her hand in mine. "But we can always come back."

She nods. "We *will* be back."

I hope she's right.

As sure as I am about the two of us, what I'm *not* as sure about is how the hell we're going to make this work beyond this week we have left together. What happens once she crashes back into reality?

Her father still wants the merger to happen.

She's going to have to deal with the fallout of running away from her wedding…from her life.

Her father will never accept me as part of his family.

But I'm not even sure she cares about that. She's made up her mind.

A sneaking fear wedges its way into my chest. Did she only make up her mind as a way to prove to her father that she's capable of making her own choices?

Did she only *choose* me because I'm the *bad boy of baseball*—representative of everything that's so completely opposite of what her brand stands for?

If she did, she did it subconsciously. I don't believe she'd ever do something like that purposely.

Either way, the fear is still there, icing over the warmth in my chest. But only when I allow it to—which is why I keep choosing to push it away.

"Should we call your mom and tell her the news?" she asks.

I nod. In the romance of getting caught up in the moment last night, we kept the news to ourselves.

But if we're going to successfully pull this off, we're going to need some help.

And my mother is the perfect person to help us. The *only* person who can help us, really.

I dial her number and put the call on speaker, setting my phone on the table between us.

"Good morning," she answers cheerfully.

Bases Loaded

"Hey, Mom," I say, and at the same time, Alexis says, "Hi Tracy!"

"Oh, I just love hearing from the two of you," she says. "How's it going up there?"

"Good." I glance over at Alexis. "Really good. I asked Lex to marry me, and she said—"

"Yes!" Alexis yells before I get the chance to get the word out. We both laugh and so does my mom.

"Oh my goodness, congratulations!" my mom cries. "I just couldn't be happier for the two of you."

I half expect her to ask about grandkids, but she doesn't.

"How did he do it?" she asks Alexis instead. "Please tell me it was in a way appropriate to share with his mother."

Alexis giggles. "It's appropriate. It was so, so romantic. He decorated the rooftop deck here at the house with all sorts of string lights, and he had soft music playing and candles everywhere...he got down on one knee at sunset and asked, and I, of course, accepted. Oh, you'll have to send her the picture," she says to me.

"There's a picture? Yes! I need to see it!"

I pull up the photo and send it right over while we talk.

"I thought you'd look shocked in that second one," Alexis says.

My brows dip. "How come?"

"Because I'd just told you I wanted to get married before Christmas Eve."

I laugh. I wasn't shocked at all. Instead, my smile was wider—because ultimately, that's what I'd been hoping she'd say.

"Wait a second," my mom says. "Before *Christmas Eve?* Like...as in *next week?*"

"Yep," we both say at the same time, and my eyes meet hers.

"Oh...my. Oh, okay. We have things to do..." she says, clearly flustered.

"We'll take care of it, Mom," I say. "And we want you to be there, of course, so we decided we'd come down to San Diego and do it there."

"You…you…you want *me* there?" She sniffles.

"Actually, if you'd officiate, that would be even better," Alexis says.

"*Officiate?* Oh, dear. Oh! Yes, of course, whatever you two want."

I can tell she's nervous even to be asked, and I think it was sweet of Alexis to think of her.

But when I think of the people who have supported us since the beginning, the list is rather short…mostly because nobody knows we're even together.

My mom. Anna. Rush and Cooper. Gregory.

That's about it.

And that's the extent of who I'd want celebrating the wedding with us, anyway.

"Mom, I have a favor to ask."

"Anything, honey," she says.

I made some notes on my calendar and have a tentative plan.

"Can you find someone to watch the boys and then book a rental with a rooftop deck with at least five bedrooms, let's say for Wednesday through Saturday?"

We'll leave here tomorrow, split the eight-hour drive into two days, and stop and stay somewhere near a winery tomorrow. Then we'll haul it down to San Diego and stay at the rental my mom secures for us. We'll spend a few days there, get married, and then head up to Disney the day before Christmas Eve.

It'll be fast, but it'll be perfect.

"Five?" Alexis echoes.

"Trust me," I say softly.

She nods.

Bases Loaded

"You got it," my mom says. "What else do you need? Clothes, flowers, food?"

I glance at Alexis, and she takes the reins on that one.

"Flowers. My mom had white and pink peonies in her bouquet, and I always wanted that, too," she says softly.

"I'll take care of it, honey," my mom says.

"I think everything else we can take care of when we're there." Alexis glances at me. "Anything else?"

I shake my head. "Thanks, Mom."

"Anything for you, baby. Listen, though. I have a little bit of news I need to share."

"What is it?" I ask, already alarmed.

She sighs. "Gregory called me last night. They were able to find some footage of you in San Luis Obispo at a gas station. I know you're way up in Carmel now, but they're on your tail if you're trying to stay out of sight. I didn't tell Gregory a single thing other than that you're both safe so he didn't indirectly lead them to you, but I just wanted to let you know."

"I think we're okay up here," I say. "California is a big state, and it took them a couple of days to find that footage. Fingers crossed it'll take a couple more to find us up here, and by that time, we'll be gone."

I hear her doorbell ringing in the background. "Oops, I better go see who that is. You two be safe. I love you."

"Love you!" we both say back, and I end the call.

Alexis's eyes are wide as they meet mine. "They traced us?"

"It's still two and a half hours away. They'll never think we're somewhere like *here*, where it's a busy town. They'll assume we went somewhere small," I say, sure I don't believe my own words.

"But now they know we're together." She sounds nervous about that, and I'm not sure what she's thinking about that.

I nod and press my lips together. "Yeah, they do. But they did anyway."

"I just don't want them bothering your mom or your sister. I don't want them involved in any of this."

"I know." I nod. "I don't, either. And even if they do, Gregory will be with them, so it'll be okay."

"I hope you're right." She doesn't sound as confident as I do. But I hope I'm right, too.

Chapter 15
Alexis

After a sexy, long morning shower together that lasts so long we actually run out of hot water, we get dressed and head into town for our marriage license.

Carmel's City Hall is a quaint little craftsman building in the heart of downtown with a shingled roof that looks more like a little house than a government building. We climb up the steps and head inside to get the paperwork rolling, and when we turn it in to the little old lady behind the desk, she eyes me up and down.

My identification has my given name on it, Caroline A. Bodega, though she narrows her eyes a little as if she *thinks* she recognize me but isn't really sure.

We pay the extra fee for the private certificate that the state of California offers, so nobody will know our business but us.

We'll tell the rest of the world when we're good and ready to make the announcement, and not a moment before.

We escape unscathed, and we've secured the first step in actually getting married.

Caroline A. Bodega and Daniel J. Brewer are set to become husband and wife as long as they do it in the next ninety days before the certificate expires.

We go back to the store in the village where I saw the dress I can't stop thinking about, and I grab my size off the rack and head into the dressing room.

That's right.

Alexis Bodega is buying a wedding dress *off the rack*.

It's not a name brand, instead hand-sewn by a local seamstress, and it's not even a wedding dress. It's a floor-length, long-sleeve gown that has a white floral pattern sewn over a blush champagne-colored lace.

When I slip it on in the dressing room and step back to look in the mirror, it's simply breathtaking.

It's romantic and dreamy, and it's perfect to set the vibe for what *I* want out of my wedding day.

It's not chiffon and silk, that's for damn sure.

It's simple and elegant, and it's just right for us.

I head up to the register to pay with some of the cash Danny handed me before I walked in.

It's weird having to borrow money from someone else when I've spent my entire adult life with plenty of money to spare.

It's a strange reminder that we should probably sign some sort of agreement going into this, but I don't *want* to. Danny doesn't need my money any more than I need his.

I know nobody ever goes into a marriage expecting it to end, but I really believe we're going to make this last forever.

And so I decide I won't bring it up at all.

The woman behind the register asks, "What event are you wearing this to?"

"My wedding," I say softly.

"Oh, congratulations. It's just stunning."

I offer a small smile as she sets the gown into a garment bag, and then I head outside to meet Danny, my smile wide as we check another task off of our to do list.

We make love yet again once we're back at the house, and then we sit on the rooftop deck and relax as we watch the sunset, holding hands and smiling as we talk softly.

We make a plan to try a local bar and grill for dinner, and it's just before we're about to head inside to get ready for dinner when Danny says, "I think we need to talk about something."

I glance over at him, and he looks a little nervous. "What is it?"

"Do, uh…should we—" He cuts himself off, and he draws in a breath. "Do we need to have some sort of agreement about assets?" He doesn't mention the word *prenup*, though I know exactly what he means.

"I wasn't going to bring it up if you weren't," I admit.

He presses his lips together. "I really and truly believe we're going to make this work, Alexis. I really do. But I had to live through the fight when my parents ended things, and they didn't really even have that many assets. And now my sister. It's just easier if the plans are all laid out in advance, you know? And I wouldn't bring it up if we were like my parents, or if we were like Anna and Chris, but the fact is…we're not. You're Alexis Bodega. You've got a fortune behind you. An entire empire. And I've got a big money contract, too, and it would be unrealistic and maybe even irresponsible not to at least have *something* in writing to protect those things."

I nod. "Okay. I think you're probably right. But do we just…" I trail off. "I don't know. Sign something for now that says all pre-marital property and assets will remain individual property during and after the marriage."

He nods. "You're good at this."

"Well, it's not my first prenup," I joke, which garners a small chuckle from Danny, though it's really not all that funny.

"That works for me. Let's add something in that we can revisit it at a later date with a lawyer."

"Sounds good." I stand to go inside and get some paper, and I return a few beats later with the pad I found in the kitchen. I spell out what we just said, and we both sign and date the paper. "I'll keep this in my purse for safe-keeping."

He takes a picture of it on his phone. "Good enough," he says. He wrinkles his nose. "That felt…wrong. I'm sorry I brought it up."

"It's what our lawyers each would've told us to do, and I want you to know that I'm not offended in any way that we did it."

"Okay. Then we should probably have sex to get that image out of my head before we go to dinner."

I laugh. "You are greedy, Mr. Brewer."

"Oh, you ain't seen nothin' yet, babe."

I giggle, and I scamper over toward the stairs to head back inside. He catches me as I get to the second step, and he pulls me into his arms and he presses his lips to mine, the awkwardness of that conversation already gone.

We're still on the stairs when he reaches down the front of my jeans and sinks a finger right inside me.

"Oh God!" I yell, and he starts finger-fucking me right there.

I reach down and rub his cock on the outside of his jeans, and he thrusts into my hand.

It's hot and sexy and a little forbidden doing this out here on this rooftop, knowing we could be seen by a nosy neighbor at any point, but I don't even care.

In fact, somehow that makes it even hotter.

Just the mere thought of what he's doing to me has me seeing stars already, and I fall apart when he slides his finger out and starts to rub my clit.

Bases Loaded

I reach into his jeans just as I start to come, and I grip onto his cock. There isn't much room to move my fist, but I slide it up and down as best I can, gripping on harder and harder as my body pulses its way through a hot climax.

His mouth is on mine, our tongues battering together as he doesn't stop rubbing away at me even though my body is coming down from the high already, and he shoves his fingers back inside me.

Oh my God. I think I'm going to come again. He pushes me right up to the edge as if he can feel me getting closer and closer and closer to exploding a second time, and then it all just…stops.

"What the hell?" I murmur.

He pulls his hand from my jeans and raises a brow. "You can wait to finish that one until I decide it's time."

My jaw drops. "Excuse me?"

He raises both brows. "You heard me."

I run my hand down his shaft and cup his balls in my hand. "You sure you want to do that when I quite literally have you by the balls?"

"God, I love you," he murmurs, and his lips crash down to mine.

I let go of his balls. I wouldn't really hurt him, but I was trying to make a point.

The ache is sharp between my thighs, and I have a feeling it will be until I'm able to come—whenever he decides it's time.

It really is just one adventure after another with this guy.

Chapter 16
Danny

It wasn't my smartest move ever.

I was seconds from bursting all over her hand when I stopped it, and now my balls ache, and my dick is begging for release.

But I can't exactly ask for a finish when I cut her off just before hers.

That wouldn't be playing fair. And neither would finishing myself off before we leave.

So I don't.

We head to the bar and grill we saw earlier today, and it's crowded—which is perfect for what I want to do. It'll allow us to blend right in.

We place our drink orders, and it's as we're perusing the menu that I slide my hand up her leg. She's in jeans since she wore the only dress she has with her last night, but that isn't about to stop me.

I already know what I'm going to order, but I slide my hand up a little higher than would normally be decent in public as I lean over and ask, "What are you getting?"

"Off, hopefully," she says, still absently perusing the menu, and I laugh.

"Are you asking?"

"I'm still a little mad that you cut me off before."

"You already had one," I point out, and I slide my finger along the outside of her jeans.

"So? I was a good girl. I deserve another." Her voice is low and whiney, and I don't know if I've ever been more grateful for another dimly lit restaurant and a circular booth toward the back. The backs of the booths are tall and the tablecloth runs down the front to block what I want to do, almost as if whoever designed this place did it with the intention of allowing people privacy.

Probably not for the activities we're about to engage in, but privacy nonetheless.

I slip my hand into her jeans and down into her panties, and her head whips in my direction. "Now?"

I raise a brow. "You basically just dared me to do it right here, right now. And who am I to back down from that?" As I say the words, I slide my finger inside her hot cunt.

She crumples back into the booth, closing her eyes as she gives in a little, and I lean down to murmur in her ear. "You have to play the part, Lex. What if people are watching us? What if they know it's you?"

Her eyes pop open, and she sits up, only having the effect of allowing my finger to penetrate more deeply.

"Oh," she gasps softly.

"I wish your tits were in my mouth," I mutter.

"So do I," she says on a groan.

"What can I get you two?" the waitress asks, appearing at the end of our table.

Alexis freezes, and I chuckle, not moving my hand from where it's currently being kept nice and warm.

"I'll take a double cheeseburger, no onion, extra bacon, and fries. And some whiskey. Carrie?" I prompt, using her given name to divert any possibility of being recognized, though the make-up and the hat seem to be doing the trick.

"Oh, uh…" she says, her voice breathless. "Chef's salad. Dressing on the side and vodka cranberry."

"Sounds great. I'll be back with your drinks in a minute," the waitress says, and she takes off to put in our order.

"You know, for someone who's going to be an Academy Award nominee next year, the acting skills could use a little work," I tease.

"Let's get you seconds from an orgasm and see how you do," she pants.

"I'm always seconds from an orgasm when I'm around you." I drop my lips to her neck and work her pussy a little harder, and her breathing kicks up a notch.

I can tell she's close.

Part of me wants to make her beg. The other part of me wants to watch her fall apart right over this table.

I settle on the latter.

She comes *hard* all over my fingers, but she manages to keep quiet as she does it, impressing me with her acting abilities all over again.

My cock begs for relief that I won't get anytime soon, but at the same time, there's a certain satisfaction in making her come over and over again. I love it. I love her. I love this life.

I don't want to leave this place.

I don't want to go back to our old life.

And in a way, we won't. We'll emerge from all this married. That's the plan, anyway—as long as we can keep off her father's radar and everything goes to plan.

I hold onto hope that it's all going to work out the way we're planning for it to.

Our food arrives quickly, and we're on our way home undetected once again a short while later.

We've just turned out of the parking lot when Alexis shocks the hell out of me by reaching across the console and massaging my cock over my jeans.

She flicks the button and lowers the zipper, and then she unbuckles her seatbelt, leans over the console, and strokes my cock a few times before she leans her head down and sucks my cock right into her mouth.

Jesus, it's pure perfection as her mouth glides up and down me, and I'm trying everything I can to focus on the road in front of me rather than on how good it feels. I need to keep us both safe, and lucky for me, traffic is light tonight.

I watch the road instead of her head, and I keep my thighs flat even though I have the urge to pump into her hot mouth.

I skid to a stop as a green light turns yellow, and I hope to God it's a long ass light.

I put my hand on the back of her head because there's really nothing hotter than holding a head down over my cock, and she takes it like a fucking champ.

She groans over me like she's enjoying this, too, and while I've had a few blow jobs in my day, this one is in some other stratosphere compared to the others. I've experienced everything from over-enthusiasm to boredom to choking to sucking too hard…but I've never experienced pure and utter perfection like I am right now.

And it's that thought that sends me flying.

I let go, leaning my head back and closing my eyes a beat as my jizz jets to the back of her throat. She keeps on sucking away, holding on, and once my body starts to calm, she pulls back and licks me clean before she leans back over to her side of the car.

It's all sorts of hot in here, and I tuck myself back in just as the light turns green.

"Well…thanks for that." My voice is hoarse and now I'm the breathless one, and she wipes the side of her mouth with her fingertips.

"Thanks for the one in the restaurant, too."

I chuckle. "Any time you need one, you just ask."

"Right back at you."

"Road head?"

"I mean…wherever. If you need it on the road, just say the word."

She giggles, and then my phone starts to ring.

We both see on the car system that it's my mom calling, and she nods toward the answer button. "Go ahead."

"Thank God she waited those five extra seconds," I say before I click answer. "Hey, Mom."

"Hey, DJ. I just wanted to let you know earlier when the doorbell rang…it was Alexis's father, the ex-fiancé, and Gregory," she says. She sounds tired.

"Oh, God, Tracy. I'm so, so sorry they bothered you," Alexis says. "I'm so sorry you got dragged into this mess."

"No, honey, don't be. I told them last I heard, you were in Santa Barbara. Gregory knew I had more info, but he played the part well. He's on your side. Both of you," she says.

My eyes meet Alexis's for just a brief moment before I return mine to the road. "Thanks, Mom," I say.

"You two be safe," she says. "They likely won't find you up north, but they were definitely looking for you. I'm not sure what happens next—if they get footage of you somewhere else or if they just go home and wait it out now. I told Mr. Bodega that if you don't want to be found to just leave you alone."

"I should reassure him that I'll be back for the Christmas Eve special," Alexis murmurs.

"Oh, he knew that. Gregory told your father that you texted him to let him know you'd be there, and he made a point of telling me that to make sure I relayed it back to you. But your dad was skeptical. He knows you two are together, and I didn't mention anything more than that."

"Thanks Mom," I say again, not really sure what else to say. It sucks she got hit up for information on us, but at the same time…she's the only person who actually knows our whereabouts.

"I'm here for you two, and I'll see you real soon, okay?"

"Yes. We're driving part way tomorrow and stopping overnight, and we'll come down to the rental the next day," I say. "I love you, Mom. Take care of yourself, okay?"

"You too. Love you guys."

"Love you," Alexis and I say at the same time, and I end the call.

Alexis is quiet as she stares out the window, and I reach over to take her hand in mine.

"Hey. It'll be okay."

She presses her lips together and nods.

"It'll all be worth it," I say softly.

I don't add that it'll all be worth it if it works out the way we want it to, but the thought still hangs in the air between us…because we don't know if it *will* work, especially not if her father and Brooks are hot on our trail.

Chapter 17
Danny

We're both up early in the morning, I think because we're checking out of this place today, and we want to spend as much time up on the rooftop deck enjoying the view together as we can before we have to go. Neither of us wants to leave.

It's the place where we got engaged, and I have a good feeling we'll be back someday—maybe to celebrate an anniversary or to bring our children here and show them the place where Mom and Dad got engaged.

I like hanging out with my nephews, but I get to send them home at the end of the day. Now, though, I have this feeling as though kids will somehow complete the picture, and it's yet another thing on my list I didn't realize I even wanted until Alexis stepped foot in my life.

I think about little miniature versions of her running around being sassy little divas, or little boys with my blue eyes, or some combination of her plus me. It's not the future I ever envisioned for myself, and I don't know how far down the road it'll be for us considering how she's in the middle of filming a movie and already has a tour planned for next year, and I have two more seasons on my contract with the Heat and I'll probably play beyond that, too.

But I see it in our future. We're still young at just twenty-eight, and maybe somewhere in our mid-thirties, we'll find the right time to make it all work.

Whatever happens, though, we'll be holding hands through it all.

I keep thinking that way. I keep the positive thoughts alive.

Because thinking ahead to Christmas Eve continually sends a knot into my stomach.

I don't know how her dad is going to react to any of this, but I can't imagine he'll approve of our marriage. If anything, I'm guessing he'll demand she get it annulled, and I have no idea how she's going to handle that.

But she's a big girl…something her father has never given her credit for being.

I won't force my own opinions and thoughts on how she should handle this onto her. She's had enough of that in her lifetime.

Instead, we'll work through it all together.

"What are you thinking about?" she asks. We're standing in an embrace by the railing, and I'm holding her against my chest as we stare out at the water hitting the shoreline. We've finished our bacon and packed our bags, and this is it. It's time to head out.

But I'm hesitating.

It feels safe here. Nobody has found us so far, and it feels like we can just stay on this rooftop, breathing in the ocean air and each other forever.

I realize how ridiculous that sounds considering the rather weighty responsibilities we have to return to, but here, life feels carefree and perfect.

"The future," I answer honestly, my chin resting on top of her head.

"What about it?"

"About how I want things with you I've never wanted before. About how I feel like we'll be back here someday."

"That's sweet," she hums as she sinks more deeply into my chest.

I tighten my arms around her. "About how we'll show our kids the place where we got engaged someday."

She pulls back out of my arms and looks up at me, her eyes a little misty at my words. "You want kids?"

"I didn't. And then I met you."

She tilts her head, and then she pushes up on her tiptoes to press a kiss to my mouth. "I love you."

"I love you, too."

I drag in a deep breath of the salty sea air, and I release it slowly, feeling instantly calmed. But my next words drag up the anxiety once more. "We should get going."

"I know."

Neither of us moves.

"I don't want to," she says.

"Neither do I."

"It just feels safe. Here in your arms, here on this rooftop. Here in Carmel. We don't know what's waiting on the other side." She's mumbling into my chest, so I literally feel her words against my body, but I feel them inside, too.

"We've got this, Lex. Together. You and me."

She nods a little and backs up, and I lean down to drop one more kiss to her lips.

"And on the other side of this road trip, we're getting married," I remind her.

Her lips tip up. "That's the only thing that could tear me from this roof."

I chuckle. "Then let's get to it."

She nods, and I take her hand as we head down the stairs. I gather the suitcases and bring them to the rental car in the garage, and then we head out.

I've just started up the car on our way to Valencia, where we'll be staying for the night, when my phone rings and we see it's my mom calling.

"Good morning," I answer.

"Hey, DJ. I heard from Gregory. I guess they traced you two up to Carmel by your rental car. They're on their way up there now."

I glance over at Alexis with wide eyes. "Oh shit."

"They'll be able to trace you now, so you need to switch cars," she says.

"But I can't reserve a new one under my name," I point out.

"Right. And I shouldn't do one under mine, either. Would Cooper or Rush help you out?"

"Definitely," I say, and I pull up the map to figure out where I can switch cars. There's a rental place ten minutes from where we are. "Thanks, Mom. I'll call you back."

It's a slight setback in our plans, but I call Cooper as I head toward the rental car facility. "Hello?" he answers right away.

"Hey, man. I need a favor, and you're on speaker."

"Hi, Alexis," he says.

"Hey, Cooper."

"What can I do for you two?" he asks.

"I need a rental car at the Monterey Regional Airport. We were traced to Carmel by my car, so I can't reserve one in my name," I say.

"Monterey? Carmel? Traced?" he repeats. "Never mind. Whatever you need, you got it. I'll do it now. What do you want and for how long?"

"Just book it for two weeks. I'll return it in LA. A truck or SUV preferably." I glance over at Alexis, and she looks nervous.

"I'll send you a picture of my license and credit card since you'll probably need to scan both at the self-service kiosk," he says.

"You're a lifesaver," I breathe.

"Nah. Just a good friend rooting for you two."

"Thanks, Cooper," Alexis says softly, and I reach over and grab her hand.

"You got it." He cuts the call to make the reservation, and I start navigating toward the airport. His details come through a few minutes later, and he really is a great friend. The best.

I drop the car on the return side and turn in the keys to an attendant, and then we head to the kiosk on the rental side to get the new car.

It's a smooth process, and we're out on the road within a few minutes.

I race the fuck out of there, sure we'll be caught…but what other choice do we have?

We either keep trying to duck from her dad, or we let him find us. And I know she wants to keep running.

She's not ready to face him yet, and I don't blame her.

I'm not ready to face him yet, either.

I'm more than happy to stay on the run with her until we no longer can. And after that…well, I suppose we'll face whatever consequences come next.

Chapter 18
Alexis

Well, if it had to happen, if we *had* to get caught, I guess it was perfect timing since we were leaving town anyway. We'll only be four short hours from Carmel, though. It doesn't feel far enough. We should've left the state. We should've kept driving. We should've found some remote location where we couldn't be traced.

But we didn't, and now we're here, on the run from my father again.

I'm sure he's thinking this is just some game to me, but it isn't. It's my life.

It's giving Danny and me this time together that we've never had before. It's bonding us closer as we start our life together.

It's allowing me to breathe when I feel like I haven't been able to for my entire adult life.

It's freeing, and it's magical, and it's…

It's starting to make me question my priorities. My goals. My dreams.

How important is a Grammy and an Academy Award in the same year, really?

It's a nice goal. A nice aspiration. But is it even *my* goal and aspiration? Or was it coded into me by my father…like everything else?

What do I really want out of life?

Because the more time I sit beside this man, the more I think…it's him. It's what we have. It's what we share. *That* is what I want out of life. More time with him. More sex. More restaurants. More showers. More kisses. More laughing. More sunsets. And maybe even…kids?

But filming, recording, touring…those are the things that will drag me away from him.

And I don't want to be away from him ever again.

I realize that's neither logical nor feasible, but this has been the best few days of my life. I'm not ready to see it come to an end.

But time barrels down on us.

We spend the night at the hotel, scared to go out in public. Scared of getting caught. Scared that somehow we'll be tracked.

Maybe by his phone. Maybe we should ditch it, but it's our one link to the outside world now. It's our way to order food, and his location is off unless we need to turn it on for any reason. And even in that case, it would take time for my father to figure out our location based on that—he'd need a warrant, or subpoenas for phone records, and all that takes time.

I'm sure the winery just up the road is beautiful. I'm sure I'd love to sample the selections in the tasting room and head out to the fields to enjoy a tour.

But fear rules me here. We just need to stay off my dad's radar for a couple more days so we can get to San Diego and get married.

Bases Loaded

I think about telling him we should move up the wedding date, but we've already got too many pieces in motion to change train tracks now.

So we put on a movie that neither of us pays attention to, and we make love, and we fall asleep early. In the morning, we head out.

We stop at some hole in the wall diner for breakfast, where we have greasy bacon and eggs, and it's fantastic. I go without make-up and a hat pulled down low, and we're able to eat undetected.

It's amazing how easy it is to blend in when I'm trying to blend in.

Nobody in here knows that Alexis Bodega is sitting in the booth by the door. Nobody in here knows that the man sitting across from me won the World Series just a few months ago. Nobody here is looking for us.

Nobody in here knows that we're on the run from my dad, and we're heading toward our secret destination wedding, and then we'll return to our lives and…

And then what?

I'll go back to filming after the new year.

He'll need to start training soon.

His season will get underway in February with Spring Training.

I'll have another album to record and then the tour to promote it and the press junket for the movie.

We'll be apart again.

I'll be stuck with my dad and Brooks again.

It's not what I want.

I let out a heavy sigh as the waitress clears away our plates.

"You okay?" Danny asks from across the table.

I lift a shoulder. "Not really."

"I know," he says. "I'm not, either."

I purse my lips. "Why not?"

"Let's talk in the car," he says, and I nod.

We get up to leave, and once we're in the car, I ask again. "Why aren't you okay?"

"Same reason you aren't. We have five days left together, and then...it's unknown."

I nod, and I reach over and touch his forearm. "I don't want it to end, Danny. I don't want to face whatever comes on Christmas Eve and after."

"I don't, either. But we'll do it together. That much I know. How do you think your dad will take the news?" he asks.

"I have no idea," I admit, and a sudden thought occurs to me. "I can't help but wonder *why* he wanted this so badly. He never mentioned it before, and then all of a sudden, it was his only focus. Forcing me to marry Brooks? It doesn't make a whole lot of sense. He never wanted to sell the company or merge or whatever. He built Bodega Talent from the ground up." I wrinkle my nose as I think through it all. Something isn't adding up, and I was too caught up in the shock of it all to question it before.

"Do you think..." he begins, but he pauses. "Nah, never mind."

My brows dip. "What?"

He seems to weigh whether or not to go ahead, and then he does—another sign to me of how much trust lies between us. "Do you think something underhanded is going on?"

I don't answer right away as I think through my answer. "Like what?" I finally ask.

"I don't know. But you think it's weird he'd want to merge. Do you think maybe Brooks is up to something?"

I think about Brooks for a minute. I've known him for a long time now, but I'm not sure I really *know* him, which was part of my reservation in marrying him in the first place. "He seems so...I don't know. Clean cut or something. I can't imagine him lurking in the background tapping his fingertips together as he plots our demise."

Danny chuckles at the image. "Yeah, you're right."

"Have you heard anything more on your dad?" I ask.

He shakes his head. "It's only been a few days. Chloe said she'd call me as soon as she had something, and maybe she just...doesn't have anything yet."

"Don't you feel like the walls are closing in on us?"

He shrugs. "We're pressed, for sure. But at least we're pressed together now. I don't see my father doing anything with that tape. I think he'll come calling for more money before he does anything, and he's been quiet the last few days."

"Doesn't that scare you?"

"Nah," he says. "Spiders scare me. My father?" He sticks out his bottom lip and shakes his head. "He's already done his worst to me. Anything else...we just deal with it."

"I guess you're right," I murmur, not as convinced as he is.

But the truth of the matter is, I can no longer act like I'm scared it'll hurt my brand.

Not when I'm doing the exact thing he has evidence of. Not when I ran out on my wedding.

Not when I'm about to marry the man I love.

Not when nobody knows where we are—something I'm shocked hasn't hit the news, which tells me my father is keeping all sorts of lies alive to protect me even though I'm certain he's furious with me.

The public will find all that out soon enough, and then that tape will be as good as garbage anyway.

We just have to get through the next forty-eight hours, and then we'll be married.

But then what?

Chapter 19
Danny

I pull into my mother's driveway nearly five hours later, and this place has always felt like home.

I let out a breath as I cut the engine, but I don't move quite yet.

Alexis glances over at me. "You okay?"

I nod slowly, my eyes fixed on the garage door in front of us. "More than okay, I think. It feels good to be here. Like we'll have an added layer of protection being close to my mom, being here in San Diego. Being in the opposite end of the state from where your dad just took off on a wild goose chase."

And with any luck, we'll have an added layer of protection because of the secret I've been keeping.

This isn't the house I grew up in, but I did grow up about thirty miles from here in Carlsbad. Every weekend, I'd hit the beach with my friends, and we managed to find whatever trouble we could. I remember a lot of bonfires, late night swimming, and hook-ups with tourists. Oh, those poor, unsuspecting tourists. It was one hell of a good time.

My mom wanted out of Carlsbad once I graduated high school, and she bought a little place in San Diego near Pacific Beach. She has city and water views since she's tucked in the slope of Mt. Soledad, and it's always a breath of fresh sea air to come visit her and stay here for a few nights.

But I won't be staying here tonight. Instead, we're stopping in to say hi, and she's going to fill us in on all the planning she's gotten done since we were last here, including giving us the address for the rental where we'll be getting married in less than forty-eight hours.

I'm ready. For all of it—but mostly to become the husband of the woman by my side.

Husband.

The word excites me rather than scares me.

"Ready?" I ask, and Alexis nods. We head up to the door, and I knock. My mom tosses it open a minute later, and she rushes into my arms.

"Thank God you're here, baby," she says. "It's so good to see you."

She squeezes me hard the way only a mother can, and it already feels safe and warm here.

She grabs Alexis into a hug next, and I can tell she feels that same sense of safety.

"I have a surprise for you both," she says, and she looks a little nervous. But then she looks at me and nods, and I know it's done. "Come on in."

We follow her in, and she closes the door behind us then leads us through the entry and to the kitchen.

And there he is.

"Gregory?" Alexis breathes. Her wide eyes dart to me, and Gregory stands.

"Ma'am," he says with a nod.

"What are you doing here?"

"I came to walk you down the aisle," he says quietly.

Alexis bursts into tears as she rushes into his arms, and my chest tightens. I could not be more grateful that she has him, and I'm so, so glad we figured out a way to get him here.

"I'm so happy you're here!" she squeals, brushing away tears as she pulls out of the hug. "But how? Aren't you supposed to be searching northern California with my dad and Brooks?"

"I told him I'd stay in San Diego and keep watch from here, and then he fired me," Gregory admits.

Whoa. That was *not* part of the plan.

"He can't do that." Her tone is adamant. "I hired you, and you're on my payroll. You're officially un-fired."

"We'll deal with the fallout after Christmas, but I appreciate that, Ms. Bodega. More than you know." He glances at my mom, and I get the very real sense that there's more to the story. Maybe we'll find out later, or maybe we won't.

"Alexis, come with me," my mom says. "The flowers arrived a little while ago and you *have* to see them. They're just gorgeous!" She leads Alexis into one of the guest rooms, and I have a moment alone with Gregory.

"Does her dad suspect anything?" I ask.

He shakes his head. "Thank you for having your mother get in touch with me. I'm happy to be part of the day."

"When I asked Alexis who she'd want there, she mentioned you. You mean a lot to her, and you mean a lot to me, too. You're the only person in her inner circle she can trust," I admit to him.

"Until she met you."

I press my lips together and nod, surprised at the strong level of emotion coursing through me at his words. "Thank you." We share an awkward moment of quiet, and then I ask, "So, uh…you and my mom, huh?"

He barely reacts, but that's pretty in line with who the guy is. He doesn't say a word. Not even a *no comment.*

I chuckle. "She'll blab to me later. Just take care of her, okay?"

He nods once. "Will do."

I'm not sure what that means, and I hope to God it isn't something sexual, but…well, fuck it. We all deserve a good railing, am I right?

My mom and Alexis return a few minutes later, and my mom gives me the address of the rental along with all the information we need to get in. Gregory and I carry the flowers, my clothes, and some bags of food to the SUV I'm driving under Cooper's name, and then we bid my mom and Gregory goodbye as we take off for our rental house.

The house she booked for us is on Mission Beach, and it fits all of the requests we had. Plenty of bedrooms for all of our guests to stay with us, a rooftop deck, and a dream of a chef's kitchen, at least according to the listing.

It's so strange to think that we're checking into this place unmarried, but we're leaving it married in a few days. The fear of what lurks behind those days is very real and tangible, but I refuse to let it mark this moment in any way. These next couple of days are going to be all about us and the love we've grown over the course of our relationship.

I pull into the tiny driveway and we both eagerly hop out of the car as soon as I cut the engine. She is as excited as I am, and nothing feels better than being on the same page.

She's right behind me as I pull the door code up on my phone and type it in, and before I open the door all the way, I turn around and drop a quick kiss on her lips.

Bases Loaded

"To the next part of our journey," I say, and she smiles as I open the door all the way.

We step in and it's even better than I could have imagined. It's a three story home right on the beach with views for days out all of the windows.

We explore the first floor which is comprised of a kitchen, the family room, an office, and a bedroom.

The second level has a couple more guest rooms and the third level is the primary suite.

Finally, we take the stairs all the way up to the rooftop deck, where we find the place where we will be married.

"This is absolutely breathtaking," Alexis says as she draws in a deep breath.

I slide an arm around her waist. It truly is breathtaking—the views, the layout of the deck, the décor, the landscaping, the woman beside me.

I draw in a deep breath, too, as I try to figure out how in the hell I got so goddamn lucky.

I have to remind myself that this is real.

I have to remind myself to stop waiting for the other shoe to drop.

But the moment we stop waiting, the moment when we start to feel comfortable…that's when shit's going to hit the fan.

Chapter 20
Alexis

I t's spectacular. The whole entire thing, and most especially the man beside me.

It's getting real as I look around at all the rooftop patio has to offer. Gorgeous potted palm trees and plants make it look lush up here, and the white travertine tiles make it look like we're on a patio leading out to the beach—which we are, only it's three stories down. The railing is made of glass to give us an unobstructed view of the beach below, and white rattan furniture with khaki-colored cushions is both neutral and beachy.

"Well, we have forty-eight hours to turn this into wedding central," Danny says as he looks around. "And it looks like it's already in pretty good shape to me."

He slips his arms around me, and we embrace as we stare out over the romantic view. The beach is right below us, but the water is a good hundred fifty feet or so away. Still, the gentle crash of the waves against the shore is both mesmerizing and tranquil.

The thought that we only have forty-eight hours should be a little daunting, but I know we can get it done between the two of us and our supporting crew. All we need is each other, really. The rest will fall into place.

Danny's phone starts to ring, breaking into the peaceful quiet up here, and he slides it out of his pocket to see who's calling.

I glance at the screen and see *Anna Banana*, and I giggle at how he has his sister labeled on his phone.

"Hey," he answers.

I can hear her voice through the line since I'm standing right beside Danny.

"TMZ is reporting Alexis as missing."

"Fuck," Danny mutters, and my heart starts to race.

It was one thing when it was just my dad and Brooks looking for us and Gregory could divert attention to help keep us off the radar. It was almost a bit of a game to duck and dodge him.

But now I'll have the entire world out looking for me, which will make it a hell of a lot harder to stay hidden.

Unless we just stay here out of sight.

I hate having to hide, but it's what I chose when I chose this career. I was aware of that, and for the longest time, I thought I would never trade my success for anything.

And yet here I am, ready to give it all up just to walk hand-in-hand with Danny into a restaurant like everybody else in the world would be able to do.

The thought makes me realize something.

It's not my *life* I want to run away from.

It's the life my father has created for me. It's my father. It's Brooks. It's what *they* want—all the shit I don't want for myself. It's what I don't just *want* to run away from. It's what I *did* run away from.

Bases Loaded

But now it feels like it's only a matter of time before we're caught.

It *is* only a matter of time before I have to return home, but I'd love to stay off the radar while I'm here.

Even the glass balcony here feels revealing.

People can just look up from the beach and see there's a wedding going on. They can zoom in on their phones to catch a glimpse of the bride and figure out where Alexis Bodega is located.

I slip inside to remain undetected.

I want to be me on my wedding day.

But now I feel like I need yet another disguise.

I head down the stairs to the family room and collapse on the couch.

Danny's voice interrupts me less than a minute later. "Hey, you okay?"

"Not really. How are we going to stay hidden, Danny?"

His lips tip up. "We're not. I have an idea."

"What idea?"

"What if you post to your socials letting everyone know where you are?"

My brows draw together. "We're trying to stay *off* the radar."

"I know. But what if you get on the radar for a minute and let people know you're fine? They'll stop looking, and we can keep our plans as they are." He looks really proud of his idea.

And honestly…it's not half bad.

I nod a little. "Can I log into my Instagram on your phone?"

"Absolutely." He hands it over, and I'm thankful I ignored all those messages about two-factor authentication.

After I log in, I glance around the room. There's a blank wall behind the couch on the other side, so I move over there. I flip the phone to the camera, select video, and start recording myself.

"Merry Christmas," I begin with confidence, and it's only now I realize that we're barreling down on Christmas very quickly here. "I heard you're out looking for me, but the good news is I'm not missing! I'm right here getting ready for the Christmas Eve special in Los Angeles. Come join me at eight PM Pacific time on NBC for some holiday magic. See you then!" I wave goodbye at the camera and cut the video.

I throw a filter on it, select Los Angeles as my location, and post without giving it too much thought, and only afterward, I wonder what my fans will think about that video.

They think everything I do is a puzzle meant for them. Sometimes I'm really just posting that I'm fine and not missing, and I want them to watch the Christmas Eve special. I hand Danny his phone back.

And then I cross my fingers that it works and stops the paparazzi and the public in general from looking for me.

But I'm Alexis Bodega, and I just ran out on a well-publicized wedding.

I should know better by now.

"Oh fuck," Danny murmurs as he looks at something on his phone.

I glance over at him, and his eyes are wide when he looks up to meet my eyes.

"What?" I ask.

"Remember how I said my dad would get in touch with me before he said anything to the media?"

My brows draw together as my chest tightens.

"I was wrong."

Chapter 21
Danny

I stare at the text from my father as I try to make sense of why he'd want to ruin our lives like this. Or *her* life, anyway. She never did anything to that asshole.

But I did.

And he's punishing *her* for what *I* did…even though I did the right thing.

Peter Brewer: *I went ahead and let my friend know she's with you just so people wouldn't be worried since she ran out on her wedding.*

"Fuck," I mutter again. I flash the screen at Alexis.

"Word is going to get out," I say.

She nods. "Then…what are we waiting for?"

My brows draw together. "What do you mean?"

"I mean…we're here to get married, and why are we putting all the things in place that really don't matter when all that matters is *us*? Let's just do it. Let's get married."

"We are, Lex. But my sister can't be here until tomorrow." The other guests, too—they're arriving tomorrow.

She glances down at the ground. "Right. Okay. Then we wait."

There's more, too—not just my sister, but Cooper is coming with Gabby, and Rush will be here.

I want my friends and my sister here as witnesses.

But Alexis doesn't have anybody coming to sit on her side of the aisle aside from Gregory.

What if we *did* do it today? Gregory is here. My mother is here. That's all we really need. We don't even have to tell anybody we did it early. If we're not caught, well, then we can still have our symbolic ceremony in front of our friends in two days.

And if we are caught...we'll be married. It won't matter. Her dad can try to force her into marrying Brooks all he wants, but legally, she won't be able to.

Legally, she'll be mine.

I dial my mom's number without saying my thoughts aloud to Alexis.

"Hey, honey," she answers.

"Can you and Gregory come over to the house?" I ask.

Alexis's head whips over to mine, and her eyes are wide.

"Right now?" my mom asks.

"Yes. Right now."

"Sure. We'll be right there," she says, and she says goodbye and hangs up.

"Right now?" Alexis breathes.

I press my lips together, and then I can't help a small smile. "Right now."

She scrambles to a stand. "Oh, uh." Her eyes dart all around the room. "What about your sister?"

"She'll be here for the next ceremony." I lift a shoulder. "This one will be just for us."

"Oh my God! I need to go get ready!"

Bases Loaded

She runs upstairs to the primary bedroom where all our clothes are waiting for us, and presumably she's getting into her wedding dress as I chuckle at her abrupt exit.

This is it.

The doorbell rings fifteen minutes later, and I peek through the peephole to see my mom standing there holding a book. Gregory has a garment bag draped over his arm—most likely my tux.

I throw the door open, and they both walk in.

"We had a feeling," she says, holding up the book that says *Officiant* on the front.

I pull my mom into a hug. "It's time."

She nods, and Gregory does, too.

"I'll head upstairs to see if she needs any help," my mom says.

"Thank you," I say, and I bend down to kiss her cheek.

That leaves Gregory and me alone, and he hands me the garment bag. "Your clothes, Mr. Brewer."

"Thanks, Greg. I appreciate it. And please, call me Danny."

"Call me Gregory," he says firmly. Then he backs it up with, "You need any help getting ready?"

It's rare he breaks character, but every time he does, I appreciate it.

I bark out a loud laugh. "I'm on it, Eagle Eye." I turn to leave, and then I turn back to Gregory. "Just so you know, my father just let the media know she's with me."

He presses his lips together. "What would you like me to do?"

"Earlier you asked me if I wanted you to take care of the problem, and I told you I'd handle it myself."

"And now?" he asks.

"I need help. I can't continue letting him hold this over us," I say. "It's not right, and we deserve freedom from the blackmail."

He nods. "Consider it done."

I stare at him, a little alarmed that it's just that easy. "What are you going to do?"

"Neutralize the threat." He punches something into his phone then slides it into his pocket.

"Is that…is that code for you're going to *kill* him?" I ask quietly.

"No!" he says, obviously a little offended that I'd insinuate that at all. "It's code for I have people in places who can…neutralize the threat. They can find the video recording and erase all traces of it."

"So when you just typed something on your phone, it wasn't a direct order to go kill the guy?" I ask.

Gregory chuckles a little. "No. I can assure you, it was nothing of that nature. I've never killed a man, and I don't have plans to start now."

"Why didn't we just do this in the first place?" I ask, my brows drawing together.

"You wanted to handle it yourself," he reminds me.

Who the fuck is this guy?

"Well, yeah. I assumed you were going to *eliminate* the threat," I admit.

He shakes his head. "Neutralize. And it's not easy, exactly. A hacker friend of mine can hack into your father's computer, his cloud, all of it, and he can erase it all."

"Erase it *all* or erase the video of us?"

He doesn't bat an eyelash at my question. "Whichever you want."

"Eh, erase it all." I shrug. "May as well pay the bastard back."

"As you wish, sir." He pulls his phone back out of his pocket and sends another message.

"Hey, Gregory?" I ask.

He glances up at me.

"Thanks, man. You're a pretty cool dude for a watchdog."

He raises a brow. "I know."

He returns his attention to his phone, and hell, if my mom *isn't* banging the guy, I'm sure I can find some lucky lady who would volunteer for that position in a heartbeat.

Chapter 22
Alexis

"Oh, honey. You are just utter *perfection*," Tracy says, and I glance in the mirror.

I did my hair and make-up myself. I can't remember the last time I did my own hair and make-up for a major event, let alone in under twenty minutes.

I've learned a few things about make-up application over the years, and I wanted a natural glow sort of look today, so that's what I did.

My hair falls in loose waves, and the dress is utter lace perfection.

I feel beautiful. I felt beautiful a few days ago when I was supposed to marry Brooks, but that was just the outer physical beauty. Today I feel right inside on top of feeling right on the outside, and that combination is what tells me this is perfect.

I'm not running anywhere today—except down the aisle toward my groom. Or…up the stairs, I guess.

"Are you ready?" she asks.

I nod, and she gives me a quick squeeze.

"Before we get this going, I just want to say thank you," she says.

"To me?" I ask, holding a hand to my chest. "I should be thanking *you*. You helped us get all this into place, and you're here officiating, and you've raised the perfect man for me..."

She presses her lips together and glances up at the ceiling before she draws in a deep breath and fans her eyes. "I knew this day wouldn't be without tears." She laughs a little. "I want to thank you for making Danny so happy. He's never been like this with a girl before, and that's what tells me this time he found the *right* girl."

I take both of Tracy's hands in mine. "Thank you for saying that. You have no idea how much it means to me."

"He's a wild one, but no matter what, he's my little boy, and I only want what's best for him. And it's so clear to me that *you* are what's best for him. So thank you for being that for my boy."

I lean in for one more hug. "I love you, Tracy," I say softly.

It feels so nice to have a parent who supports us and our dreams—but really and truly the dreams we have now, not the dreams we had back when we were teenagers.

Dreams change.

Goals change.

Feelings change.

But the love I have for Danny...that's solid. It may shift and transition through the years when I see him as a dad, or when I see him as he retires, or when I see him old and gray, but those are the shifts and transitions that will draw us closer together as we navigate this life together.

"If you're ready, I'll send Gregory up," she says.

I nod, feeling a little misty. "I'm ready."

She smiles one more time, and then she leaves.

I'm alone for a beat, and I allow my mind to wander.

Bases Loaded

Is it wrong to do this without my father here?

No.

Is it wrong to do this without any friends here?

No.

Ultimately this is my life merging with Danny's, and this is what we want. Social norms and expectations can fuck right off.

Two short raps at the door tell me Gregory is here.

"Come on in," I yell.

The door opens, and Gregory walks in. He stops short by the door when he glances up and sees me. "Ms. Bodega, wow. Ma'am, you look so..." He pauses as he searches for the right word. "Happy."

"I *am* happy." I smile softly, his single word meaning the entire world to me.

"What a road this has been," he murmurs.

"Thank you for all your help in getting me here. I don't say it nearly enough, Gregory, but I appreciate you so much. I'm so thankful you're a part of my life, and more often than not, you're like a father to me."

"I'm thankful to be a part of it. I know I don't mention it often, either, but I once had a daughter who was a lot like you. Smart as a whip. Talented. Sassy. Beautiful. I lost her far too young, but when I started working with you, it healed a little part of me that died with her. I couldn't protect her, but I *can* protect you."

"Oh, Gregory," I cry, and I rush into his arms for a hug. "Thank you." I draw in a shaky breath as I do my best to compose myself.

"You ready for this?" he asks.

"I'm ready."

"Then let's go get you married."

We head upstairs to the rooftop, and when he opens the door, I see how it has been transformed. Danny must have gotten dressed in two seconds flat and then rushed up here with the flowers and the beautiful arch he put together for us to stand beneath as his mother marries us.

I see a tripod with Danny's camera set up on it—our very own video recording of our special ceremony.

And standing under the arch is our officiant and her son, the man about to become my husband.

In a tux.

That's right.

Daniel James Brewer is wearing a tuxedo, and he looks fine as *fuck*.

I take Gregory's elbow as I walk across the deck toward them to the soundtrack of the ocean. We stop when we get to the end, and Gregory places my hand in Danny's.

"You shaved," I murmur.

"You're gorgeous," he says, and his eyes are heated as they land on me and don't move—as if he can't look away.

I can't look away from him, either.

Tracy asks, "I'm thrilled to be here today to celebrate the union of Daniel James Brewer and Caroline Alexis Bodega, two people very special to me, Gregory, and each other. Today, you stand before us, ready to declare your lifelong commitment to one another. Danny, what would you like to vow to Alexis today?"

Danny draws in a deep breath and offers a chuckle. "Well, I thought I had another forty-eight hours to write this speech, so I guess I'm speaking from the heart today."

All three of us laugh at his words. It's rushed, but you know what? There are no other words I'd want to hear from him right now than those directly from his heart.

He turns toward me and takes my hands in both of his. "Before I met you, I wasn't interested in a long-term relationship. My life was baseball and that's all I cared about.

Bases Loaded

And then one of my best friends told me to name the one woman who I'd want to be with if I could with no consequences, and my answer was immediate."

His hands squeeze mine.

"Alexis Bodega. It had nothing to do with the fact that you are gorgeous, though you are. But that's just surface level. I was always intrigued by you and impressed by your incredible talents, and then we were lucky enough to be in the same room at the same time when you came to sing at our opening day celebrations."

He pauses, and I think back to that day. I was so nervous to be in the same room with all those incredible ballplayers, but I had no idea that the future held *this* for me.

"It was everything to me to meet the girl of my dreams, and my life hasn't been the same since that moment. Every single day I've known you, I have fallen deeper in love with you. From the text messages while you were on tour that helped us form a friendship that would become the base foundation of where we're at today all the way until the present day, where I can't picture my life without you, every day has been an adventure. Every day has been a blessing. And today, I promise to protect you when you need protection. I promise to love you. I promise to care for you. I promise to hold you close. I promise to fight to be with you every single day. I promise to run away with you—*always*. I promise to treat you like you deserve to be treated. I promise to give you the space to be who you are, and I promise to support you in the choices you make. I'll be strength when you're weak, courage when you're scared, and energy when you're tired. But most of all, I promise to love you from now until my dying breath."

His vows are not just the makings of some beautiful song lyrics. They're everything to me.

I thumb away a tear that splashes onto my cheek. I'm not sure how I'm supposed to follow that up. I'm used to crafting lyrics and using words, but I haven't really had time to think about what I want to say today.

So I guess, much like him…I'll just speak from the heart.

"They say you meet the one when you're not looking, and I can assure you that I was not looking. I felt like something was missing from my life, but I assumed it had more to do with my career than my heart. But that was only until my heart was lucky enough to find you. I remember walking into the clubhouse on opening day. I was terrified—not to sing in front of the crowd gathered there on opening day but to be in the presence of so many of baseball's greats, only to be introduced to the man who would become my husband a mere nine months later. I never could've seen my life taking this course nine months ago."

I shake my head a little as I try to come to grips with the fact that this is real.

"I never could have imagined how you'd make every single one of my dreams come true. Being with you is more thrilling than being in front of a crowd of thirty thousand people. It's more exciting than being nominated for an award. I would run away with you every day for the rest of my life if it meant I got one more minute with you, Danny. I never knew love like this existed, and that's how I know what we're doing today is right. I know you love me because I *feel* it. It's genuine and true and perfect. It's us lifting each other up, supporting each other, and being there for each other in all the ways that matter. I promise to support you and your dreams. I promise to honor you and cherish you. I promise to communicate with you even when it's hard, and I promise to stay up and fight instead of going to bed mad. But most of all, I promise to love you from now until my dying breath."

He squeezes my hands still held in his, and his lips tip up in a small smile. *I love you*, he mouths to me.

I love you, I mouth back.

We both turn to look at Tracy.

"Danny, do you take Alexis to be your wife, to commit to only her through whatever life may throw at you until death parts you?"

Danny turns his gaze from his mom to me. "I do."

My smile is so wide that my cheeks hurt.

I love the wording of that—it encompasses the traditional vows of *to have and to hold through sickness and health* and all that with the simple phrasing of *whatever life may throw at you*.

We both turn back to Tracy at the sound of her voice.

"And Alexis, do you take Danny to be your husband, to commit to only him through whatever life may throw at you until death parts you?"

"I do," I say solemnly, and it's his turn to smile.

"Then let's exchange rings and make this official. The ring is a symbol of the never ending love and commitment you share, and the rings seal the promises you've just made. Danny, please place the ring on Alexis's left ring finger and repeat after me."

Danny pulls the band he bought at the jewelry store in Carmel out of his pocket, and he poises it halfway down my finger.

"I give you this ring as a symbol of my commitment and love," Tracy says.

Danny repeats the words, and then he slides the simple eternity band all the way down snugly onto my finger.

He hands me the ring he bought for himself, too, and I poise it over his finger then repeat the words Tracy says.

"I give you this ring as a symbol of my commitment and love." I slide it down firmly onto his finger. I know he'll have to

131

take it off during games. He can't grip a bat with a piece of metal on his hand, but I know the commitment will still be in his heart.

"It is my wish that your marriage, your trust, and your love will grow even stronger with time," Tracy says, and she brushes a tear from her cheek. "By the power vested in me by the state of California, it is my honor to declare you husband and wife. Danny, you may kiss your bride."

He pulls me into his arms and plants a good one on me, and that's it.

We're married.

We're *married*.

Chapter 23
Danny

H oly shit.
We're married.
I'm a *husband.*
I have a *wife.*

"Congratulations," my mom says once I pull back from the kiss that might've turned indecent if my mother wasn't here. She hugs me, squeezing me tightly, while Alexis hugs Gregory, and he says a similar sentiment to her. "I'm so happy for you."

"Thanks, Mom. For everything."

She brushes away some more tears, and she hugs Alexis next while Gregory sticks out a hand to shake mine.

I bat it out of the way and give him a hug, too. He's surprised by me, but I kind of like throwing this guy off his game a little. "Thanks for everything, Sargeant Sunshine."

He muffles a chuckle, but I swear I saw it there. "You're welcome," he says gruffly.

My wife plows into me. "Oh my God, we're married!"

"We're married," I echo. That'll take some getting used to.

Gregory grabs the four flutes and a bottle of champagne, and he pops it open. He pours the liquid out, only putting a small sip into his own, and then he hands us each a glass for a toast. "To the newlyweds," he says, and we all clink glasses.

Before I take a sip, I drop a kiss down to my wife's lips, and then we each drink some of the champagne.

Gregory stops the recording on my phone and readjusts the tripod, and he acts as an amateur photographer to snap the most important day of our lives for us on my phone.

It's not the wedding most people would expect for Alexis Bodega, but somehow, it's absolutely perfect for us.

And now we have five days to enjoy being newlyweds.

Five days until she has to return to reality…with me by her side. With *her husband* by her side.

My mom signs our marriage certificate, and Gregory and my mom leave after the glass of champagne. They don't make a big production out of it, instead clearly getting the hint that the two of us would like some time alone to celebrate our union.

I click play on "Come Away with Me" by Norah Jones. My usual playlists tend to be eclectic, but not full of romantic songs. Still, the first time I heard this one, it hit me in its simplicity. It's all I want—for the two of us to be able to go away together, relying solely on each other, just as we have for the last few days.

I don't know if anything could have pushed us closer together than her showing up at my hotel room and asking me to run away with her.

When she said *run away with me* and I said *always*, I meant it.

We sway to the song on our rooftop patio, her head against my chest. The moment feels like utter perfection, unmarred and uninterrupted, a moment just for the two of us to share.

Tomorrow our guests will start arriving. They'll be expecting to watch us get married the next day.

Bases Loaded

We don't have to tell them it's already done. This was our own plan, our own measure of protection against any outside forces who might show up between now and then.

And I'm ready to make it official with the *consummation*.

The song ends, and another song starts to play, this one by Adele.

I filled the playlist with romantic tunes, and one or two by her even made the list against my first instinct that I didn't want to play a song she might have written for someone else.

But I reminded myself that there *was* no one else before me. She's made that clear, just as there was no one else for me before her.

And there will be no one else after her, either.

This is it. The two of us, sealed in commitment, forever.

I wouldn't have involved my mother as our officiant if I didn't really believe we were going to find a way to make this work.

She pulls back as we listen to Adele croon about always loving you, and her eyes meet mine.

"We did it," she whispers as her eyes search mine.

"We did."

She must find what she needs as her gaze lingers on mine, and she rises to her tiptoes to meet my lips in a kiss.

Our kiss intensifies, turning urgent as she feels the same need I do, that same desire to start our forever right now. I pull back and I take her hand in mine. I lead her down the stairs to the primary bedroom, and we kiss some more in there before I painstakingly slowly lower the zipper on her dress and help her out of it.

It falls to a pile on the floor, and she stands in front of me in a lacy white lingerie set—a true fantasy come to life.

How the fuck did a guy like me get so lucky?

I get even luckier as she unwraps me like a present. She slides my tuxedo jacket off my shoulders, and it drops to the floor. She pulls off my tie then gets started on the row of buttons down my shirt, and once she gets to the last one, she slides her hands along my abdomen before moving them around me to pull me close. We kiss some more, our hands exploring each other as if it's our first time, and in a way it *is* our first time. We've never done this as husband and wife before.

There's a new level of emotion between us that didn't exist before.

I didn't think it would feel this different this fast, but it does. We're bonded in a way now that neither of us has ever been bonded to another person before, and while that easily could've been said about the two of us before the last hour, this is different.

Before we still had the threat of all the other shit falling down around us to tear us apart.

But now…we're safe. We're protected by the promises we made.

They can try to come at us with their manipulations and their lies, but they won't break us. And there's an awful lot of comfort in that.

I turn us and back her up until her legs hit the bed, and then I gently lower her down, kissing her the entire way. I break the kiss to climb up and hover over her for a beat.

"I love you, my wife," I murmur, my eyes on hers, and the way she's looking up at me with pure trust combined with heat and lust nearly makes me lose it.

"I love you, too, my husband," she says, rolling the word around a little, and it's absolute music to my ears—not just because her voice is naturally melodic, but because more beautiful words have never been spoken.

I slide her panties down her legs, and she sits up to take off her bra while I shove my pants and boxers off.

I move over her again, and this time as our eyes connect, I push into her.

My chest is tight with emotion as I move slowly at first, her tight pussy pulsing over my cock. She moans, and I bury my face in her neck as our bodies speak the language they know so well.

I groan at the perfect feel of her, my voice humming against her throat as I inhale, breathing her in.

Her nails run along my back, and when I buck into her a little harder, her nails start to dig. Every thrust is another promise that this is forever, and I feel it in my heart as I make love to her.

My need grows unbearable, and I pick up the pace as urgency starts to set in. I want her to come at the same time as me, to start our life in perfect synchronization, and I feel her cunt start to clench around me as her moans get louder and more heated.

"Come with me," I growl into her throat, and she gasps at my words.

I start to drive into her with desperation, and I move away from her neck to capture her lips with mine. The heat builds until it breaks, ripping through me in a soul-shattering kind of orgasm. She cries out as I start to come. Time stands still as we continue moving in unison, and our bodies give way to the brutal climax we've been racing toward.

Her nails dig into my back as we crash through the waves of pleasure together, an explosion that rocks us both to our very cores together. Eventually the pulses start to slow, giving way to the sweet afterglow that I want to bask in forever.

We're both quietly panting as we catch our breath after that brutal release, and I pull out of her and lay beside her.

"Married sex takes the cake as the best sex," I say, and I offer my hand for a high-five.

She laughs as her hand slaps mine.

LISA SUZANNE

I think I might be able to get used to this whole newlywed thing.

Chapter 24
Alexis

We spend a large majority of the rest of the night and the next morning naked, but then our guests are going to start showing up, so we only have a few more minutes before we have to get in the shower and put some clothes on.

"Are we going to let everyone in on our secret?" I ask softly as I trace little circles on his chest.

"Depends. Do you want to go through with the whole thing again for their sake or just tell them the truth and have a two-day party?"

I chuckle. "Two-day party for sure. Who did you invite?"

I know everyone is staying here, which is why Danny wanted a big house for this. But what he didn't tell me is *who* he invited.

"I kept it really small. Gregory was the main surprise. I invited Cooper, Rush, and Anna, too. I guess her soon-to-be-ex is taking my nephews for the weekend so Anna could come party it up with us. And Gabby's dad is taking in their little girl while they come here for a quick getaway."

"But this means no more naked time?" I ask, and he laughs.

"Naked time is always encouraged. We can come up to our bedroom any time for as much naked time as you want."

I giggle, and then we take our shower together.

Gregory and Tracy are the first guests to show up, and they come by at lunchtime with their suitcases and some food for us.

"Hope you two had a fun night," Tracy says lightly, and I blush furiously while her son doesn't bat an eyelash.

"Hope you and the RoboCop had a fun night, too," Danny says.

"That's a new one," Tracy says, and Danny shrugs.

"Trying some new nicknames out. The Punisher? Stone Cold Greg? He seemed to like Sargeant Sunshine."

Gregory doesn't bat an eye at all the nicknames. He doesn't react at all, which makes it even funnier to me.

We eat lunch together, and then the doorbell rings. Gregory gets up to answer it just to ensure it's not any sort of threat, and I have to admit, I like having him close.

A minute later, Anna and Rush walk into the kitchen.

I leap out of my seat to give my sister-in-law who doesn't actually know yet that she's my sister-in-law a hug while Danny greets Rush with a bro hug and a slap on the back.

"I'm so happy you're here!" I squeal.

I always wanted a sister. I always wanted a *sibling*—someone to share the ups and downs with, to complain about Mom and Dad to, someone who would miss Mom once she was gone as much as I did. It was hard facing that loss with my father, who had just lost a wife. It's not the same thing.

A little girl needs her mom.

She needs her dad, too. But her dad started to turn on her somewhere along the way, and she never even saw it coming.

Bases Loaded

If Mom was here, I can't help but wonder how different my life would be. Same question for a sibling. Would either of them have been able to manage my father better than I did?

Maybe I did something wrong along the way that led him to where he is now. Or maybe none of it has anything at all to do with me, and it's all on him.

I think somehow I managed to end up right where I'm supposed to be. I just wish I could've ended up here with my dad's blessing.

I have Gregory's, though, and that's good enough for me.

"So what's the big secret?" Anna asks.

I glance over at Danny. "You didn't tell her why she needed to come here?"

He shrugs. "I figured the fewer people who knew, the better."

"Including your own *sister*?"

Anna laughs. "That's Danny for you. I mean, I have an idea of what it might be, but…"

"Well, we have some news," Danny says dryly. He nods at me as if to tell me to go ahead.

"We were planning to get married on Saturday, but we did it yesterday and now we're going to party for the next two days," I blurt.

Anna's jaw drops open, and Rush has a similar reaction beside her.

"You're married?" Anna breathes.

"Holy shit, man," Rush says, and he bro slaps Danny on the back again. "Congratulations!"

"My sister-in-law is Alexis Bodega?" Anna says. "My sister-in-law is Alexis Bodega. Oh my God, I need to sit."

I giggle at her reaction, but she does, in fact, sit, as she fans her face.

"I mean…I had a feeling that's what this was, all top secret and everything, but to actually hear the words, and it's already done. Wow. Wow! I'm just…I'm—I didn't think Danny would *ever* really get married, and now he *is*, and to *you*, and wow!"

"Say *congratulations*," Danny teases.

She jumps up. "Congratulations!" She pulls me into her arms and gives me a big squeeze, and she hugs Danny next while Rush grabs me up into a big hug.

This is the sort of family I wish I had grown up with. Maybe I wasn't lucky enough to grow up with this, but I have it now, and I won't waste a single day. I will hold onto the gratitude I feel in this moment forever.

Cooper and Gabby arrive next, and they have a similar reaction. Nobody can believe that Danny, the bad boy of baseball, eternal bedhopping playboy, is *married*.

And furthermore, nobody can believe that he snagged Alexis Bodega.

But in all honesty, I feel like I'm the lucky one.

We spend the rest of the day eating, drinking, and drinking some more as we celebrate this new union. Once it gets dark outside, Tracy decides to head out to give *us kids* some privacy even though we tell her to stay.

And Gregory actually says, "I think you're in safe hands here, so I will leave you to your party."

He heads out with Tracy, and I have no idea if he's staying at her house or what's going on there…but *something* is definitely going on there.

We head down to the beach, and Danny starts a bonfire, where we roast marshmallows and we're hidden by the dark of night.

Nobody walking along the beach knows it's Alexis Bodega partying with three of the hottest baseball players who just won the World Series.

Bases Loaded

Nobody knows I'm married to Danny Brewer now.

Nobody knows I'm Mrs. Caroline Alexis Brewer.

That has a damn nice ring to it, and part of me can't wait to tell the entire world.

Chapter 25
Danny

The bonfire is exactly the sort of relaxing atmosphere Alexis and I have been craving. Being out in public with the people we're closest to feels incredible, and I don't really know how many opportunities to do this sort of thing our future will hold.

I hope it's a lot.

I fear it's not.

We're sitting in camping chairs we found at the house in a circle around the small fire. We're talking about everything and nothing—memories of bonfires as kids, or of the beach, or of family vacations. It's a rare moment of peace when we get to just sit and relax with friends, in particular in this sort of environment. Here we're just six normal people, and there's something really great about that.

Cooper and Rush are two of the most chill guys I know. Gabby is a sweetheart, and Anna is...well, she's my older sister.

Bossy and obnoxious, but it's awfully nice to have her here. And it's even better seeing her forming a bond with my wife.

Jesus. I'm still not used to saying that…but I think I'll get used to it pretty quickly considering every time I look at her, the words run through my brain.

Anna asks Alexis a question about the dress she wore, and Alexis asks to borrow my phone. The three ladies move over to sit on one side of the fire as they begin looking through all the photos from yesterday while I sit with Coop and Rush.

"What's it like being married?" Rush asks.

"Sort of like dating, but with less sex, I'd imagine," Cooper quips, and I chuckle.

"So far that does not seem to be the case for me." I smirk, and they both laugh. I turn to Cooper. "When are you and Gabby going to make things official?"

"When we got engaged, we always said we'd figure out our date in the off-season, and while neither of us is in any sort of rush, we'd like to make it official before the season starts."

"Before the season starts? We have to be back for spring training in two months," I point out.

That reality plows into me.

It's not just that this dreamland we've found ourselves in is going to end in a few days when she has to go perform on Christmas Eve, but then we're back to reality. She gets back to filming. A month and a half later, I travel to Arizona for spring training. It feels like the beginning of the end of the bliss where we have this unlimited time together, and I'm not ready for reality to come crashing in just yet.

I try to put it out of my mind, but it looms there, growing bigger and stronger by the minute.

The fire crackles in front of us, the flickering flames casting glows on the faces of my friends.

Cooper clears his throat. "Yep. We've decided on the last weekend in January. We're keeping it small, and invitations will go out around the first of the year. But if you can, both of you…keep that weekend clear." He glances over at me and takes a quick sip of beer. "And while we're on the subject, would you be my best man?"

"Not Troy?" I ask, surprised he's asking me.

"He'll be busy being father of the bride." Cooper shrugs.

"Of course, man. I'm honored you asked." I hold my can up, and he hits mine with his.

"Well now I just feel left out," Rush jokes, and we both laugh. "But since we're on the subject…" He glances over at Anna, who is deep in conversation with the girls about the gorgeous dress Alexis wore yesterday. He looks back at me and draws in a deep breath before he lowers his voice. "I want to ask your sister to marry me. I don't need your dad's approval, but I do need yours."

My brows rise—and my hackles, too, at the mention of my father, who I never responded to earlier. I push that out of my head as I focus on Rush's question. "You…you need mine?"

"I know it's fast, but I see how happy you are with Alexis." He glances at Cooper. "And you with Gabby. And I don't know. I guess I just…I want that, too. I want to be a permanent part of not just her life, but the boys, too. I want her there when I get home."

"Wow." I take a sip of my beer because it *is* the brother's job to make the potential future husband sweat a little, right?

But I know Rush, and even though my first instinct when I heard they were together was to tell him *hell* no, I see the way he is with Anna.

And I've seen how Anna was with Chris.

This is a much, much better fit than that ever was.

My sister is *happy*. She's relaxed with him. She smiles more. She's still stressed with the boys, and overwhelmed, but Rush is the kind of guy who will help guide her through that and make her load lighter.

"Of course, man. I'm honored you asked. Congratulations. Well, congratulations if she says yes."

Both Rush and Cooper laugh, and this is the life.

My two best friends here with me as the three of us found something not a single one of us was looking for.

I guess that's what happens when the right woman comes crashing through the barrier into our hearts. It doesn't matter if we're looking or not. If she's the right one, she'll find her way in.

We stay out until midnight, the legal time when bonfires have to end, and then we head inside, where all the couples split off to go to their own respective bedrooms.

Tomorrow was supposed to be our wedding day, and it's crazy to me that it already happened. As I make love to my wife before we go to bed, I can't help but think that this really is the life.

In the morning, though, things start to fall apart at the seams.

Chapter 26
Alexis

"Mm," I moan. I've never actually woken up to a massage before, but he's working my back like a pro, and once I'm lucid enough to realize what's happening, I flip over so he can massage my *front*, too.

We fell asleep naked, and he takes full advantage of that as I turn toward him, massaging my breasts now instead of my back.

"Oh God," I moan. I can feel myself getting wetter and wetter just from the work he's doing on my chest and a fierce ache forms between my legs.

Instead of moving on top of me, though, he settles in on his back and urges me on top of him. I straddle him, but he doesn't push into me quite yet. Instead, he grabs my ass and one of his fingers moves over a little to press on my asshole.

I lean forward—maybe to give him better access, or maybe to feel his cock as it throbs between us.

"What are you doing?" I whisper, and he pushes his finger in.

"Exploring my wife's body."

I cry out louder than I probably should given the fact that there are other people in this house, but I don't really care. We're newlyweds, and we're enjoying our private time together, and hearing him call me his wife with his finger moving into that forbidden entrance nearly sends me into an instant climax.

He slowly fills me as he moves his finger up, and it's a little unexpected, but it's new and different and freaking out of this world. I gasp as he pulls his finger out then thrusts it back in, stretching the tight hole, and my hips shift back as I moan my pleasure. I shift back far enough that he fists his cock in his free hand, his other hand still tied up with my ass, and I slide down on top of him.

Holy shit.

I claw at his chest as I feel the fullness from both ends, and he helps guide me up and down with one hand on my ass cheek while the other continues to drive in and out of my ass.

I slide up and down his cock, and he slides up and down my ass.

I'm not sure I can take much more before I completely fall apart, and just when I think I'm about to come, he slips his finger out of me.

"Flip over," he demands, and I do it, getting up on all fours.

He slides his cock back into me from behind, and he slips his finger back into my ass, working both entrances at the same time from a different angle.

My nipples graze along the soft comforter, sending new shockwaves through me as I shift my hips back to urge him in deeper.

Every thrust sends me closer and closer to the edge, and then my body can't take any more of the onslaught of pure pleasure.

The intensity of this climax is like nothing I've felt before as it radiates from three different pleasure points. I scream my way through it as my body vibrates and pulses through the tidal wave of bliss, and he doesn't pull his cock or his finger out of me until I collapse down on the bed, unable to physically hold myself upright any longer.

He pulls out of me and fists his cock, letting out a low growl as he jerks himself off, the hot come splashing down onto my ass with every jerk of his hand, and when he's done coming, he rolls his dick around in the mess he just made on my ass for a beat before he lets out a long sigh and stands. He returns a beat later with a towel, and he wipes me clean.

It's sort of a strange thought, but it runs through my brain anyway. I would've left it there all day, knowing that he marked me as his.

What we just did was hot and primal and so, so damn good.

I'm panting, unable to move, and he leans down and presses a kiss to my temple.

I think I fall asleep for a bit, and I wake when he walks out of the bathroom with a towel around his waist.

"What a way to wake up," he says, and a lazy smile pulls at my lips as I flip over and check out *my husband* wearing just a towel.

"Mm-hm," I murmur. That's right…those abs are mine.

I might just be the luckiest girl in the world.

He picks up his phone off the nightstand and glances at the screen.

"Oh shit," he says. He glances up at me. "We have a problem."

"What's wrong?" I ask.

"Fuck. Actually, we have two problems. A text from my father that says I have until noon today to reply to him and a text from Gregory that says your dad is headed back to San Diego."

"Shit," I mutter, and I force myself to sit up. I feel a little dizzy after that ridiculous sexual encounter I just had, and it takes me a minute to get my bearings.

"Are you okay?" he asks.

"It just feels like we can't catch a break." I let out a heavy sigh. "Let's tackle one thing at a time. What does your father want?"

He shrugs. "No idea. I never replied to him yesterday, and it would appear he's unhappy about that."

"Well, start there. Let's find out."

He nods and dials his father—still in his towel. He sits on the edge of the bed and runs a hand through his wet hair as he puts the phone on speaker so I can hear, too.

"I figured that would get you to call," his father answers. No *hello*. No cordial greeting. Just an asshole response from a total jerk.

"What do you want from me?" Danny asks.

"You know what I want," he hisses.

"More money? Fine. Take it all. I don't even fucking care anymore."

"I don't want your money. You ruined my life, and now, well…" he trails off, but the insinuation is clear. He wants revenge, and he doesn't care that it's his own son he's getting revenge on.

"I didn't ruin your life," Danny protests. "*You* did that with the choices you made."

He's facing away from me, but I give him a silent *way to go* pat on the back.

"And you took those choices and used them to ruin me," his father says.

"What is your problem?" Danny asks. "Why are you doing this to me now?"

"Because I have the leverage to do it now. I've waited nearly twenty years for this moment."

"What, the moment when you could try to take it all out from under me? Or the moment when you know you're dying from the cancer eating away at your lungs, and you won't have to face any other consequences than burning in hell once your number's called?"

His father is silent on the other end of the line.

"Yeah. I know about it. And I have other shit on you, too, so you can fuck right off." Danny hangs up on his dad, and he hunches over, leaning his elbows on his knees and hanging his head for a beat.

I get onto my knees and move over toward him, linking my arms around him for a bear hug from behind.

"Are you okay?" I ask quietly.

He blows out a heavy breath. "Fine," he mutters.

"Talk to me."

"I didn't want to use that against him. I just…felt like I was out of cards to play, and it just tumbled out."

"I know it did. And now we wait for his reaction."

He turns around to look at me, and he presses a soft kiss to my lips. "I'm sorry if I just made things worse for us."

I shake my head. "Don't you dare be sorry. I'm sorry you're dealing with this. I'm sorry he treats you like that."

He shakes his head. "It's not your fault. And I have Gregory working to erase that tape, so fingers crossed it works, and he won't have a threat to hold over us anymore."

"If you have Gregory on this, I'm confident we'll be free of him soon. He's the best," I say.

"He is. Do you know what's going on with him and my mom?" he asks.

I shake my head. "He doesn't talk to me about anything personal. The closest we got to personal stuff was before he walked me down the aisle, and he said he thinks of me like a daughter."

"I love that for you," he says softly.

"Me too. I think he'd be good for your mom. They seem like such opposites, but I think they could make each other happy."

"So do I," he murmurs, and then he rises to a stand. "Okay, next on the agenda is your dad. What are we going to do?"

"How did he trace us to San Diego?"

He shrugs as he walks over to grab some clothes from his suitcase. "I'm guessing it had something to do with Cooper and Rush coming to town, but I'm not sure. It was risky to let anyone know where we are."

I nod. "Maybe Gregory could get us a new car and we could duck out early?"

"Do you *want* to duck out early?"

I shake my head. "Of course not. This is pure heaven here. And the bonfire last night? I've never done anything like that. I loved it, Danny."

"Then we come back and we do it again. Do you still want a honeymoon at Disneyland?"

I nod. "Yes, but it was supposed to be in two days."

"It still will be, but we might have to be on the run for those two days in between," he says.

It feels like it's just one complication after the next.

I want his dad to leave us alone.

I want my dad to leave us alone.

I want the world to leave us alone.

But I don't get to have any of those things. The only solution if I want to be alone with this man is to keep running.

"Then let's run," I say.

Chapter 27
Danny

"Neither of us wants to leave," I announce at breakfast. "But her father has traced us here to San Diego again, so we have to go. Gregory is bringing us a new car in a bit, and Cooper, if you can take the one under your name back to the airport, that would be a big help."

Concerned eyes stare back at me, and I can't help but think how much I appreciate everyone in this room.

And I'm so goddamn glad we already went through with the wedding. If we hadn't, we'd be waiting on today, and we wouldn't be married yet, and we'd be scrambling to get the hell out of here.

But now, we're together. We're in this. We're eating up every last second we can of being together before the world comes crashing back down on us.

Cooper nods. "You got it, man. Anything else we can do?"

"Have fun here at this place and take care of checkout. Otherwise, I think we're just…on our own," I say.

I glance over at Alexis, who nods.

Part of this is adventure—the fear of getting caught, the unknown of what awaits us on the other side.

But the other part—that's pure love. It's creating a bond that no one else will ever be able to break. It's creating memories of our first days as a married couple.

I wonder how many other newlyweds can say they were on the run from the wife's father the first few days they were married.

It sounds ridiculous when I think about it, but it's our reality. If we want these quiet moments together without interference from a man who essentially kept this woman prisoner with her unknowing consent, then this feels pretty much like our only option.

"Where should we go?" I ask Alexis as we throw our stuff into our suitcases after breakfast.

She shrugs. "I'd say south to Mexico, but we don't have our passports."

"Then our option is fairly limited to going north. Or to Vegas."

She raises her brows. "We could go to Vegas. It might be fairly easy to get lost in the crowd there, and I feel like he'd never actually look at your house."

"Our house now, babe."

"Our house," she amends. "But I still feel like that's dangerous."

"What about Palm Springs?" we both say at the same time, and then we both laugh.

It's a bit out of the way to the east—as in a couple hours out of the way, but it would give us a place to go for the next couple of nights to keep us off the radar, and then we could hit Disneyland on our final day off the radar.

We say our goodbyes to Cooper, Gabby, Rush, and my sister, and I can't help but wonder when we'll all be in the same room again and what will be different.

Will it be at Cooper's wedding next month? Will Rush and Anna be engaged by then?

Will it be this calm and laid back? Or will it be riddled with the fanfare that comes along with both our chosen careers?

Time will tell.

We pack an SUV Gregory dropped off for us with our belongings and most of the food in the kitchen so we don't have to worry about getting food. We head toward Palm Springs, and my mom texts the details for yet another house she rented for us.

It's been a whirlwind few days, and I can't thank my mother enough for all she's done to help us out.

And Gregory. And Cooper.

It's a tight network of close allies, and I'm appreciative of all we have.

I pull up the address my mom sent us, and we discover it's nestled in the boulders of Rock Reach in Yucca Valley, a forty-five minute or so drive from Palm Springs. It's also highly secure—something we didn't ask for but we both need.

We get into the house without a problem, and we find floor-to-ceiling panoramic views of the desert out the window. It's gorgeous, and there's a pool out back. It's chilly this time of year, but the notebook on the kitchen counter tells us the pool is heated and ready for our use.

I didn't bring a swimsuit.

Neither did she.

Sounds perfect to me.

Just after we haul all our shit into the house, my phone starts to ring, and I see it's Cooper calling.

"Hey, we just got to our new place," I answer.

"Alexis's dad was just here," he says.

"What?"

"He showed up here."

"What did he say?" I ask.

"He demanded to know where his daughter was, and he cased the joint trying to find her as if we were hiding her here."

"Jesus, man. I'm sorry." I glance up at Alexis, who looks like she's about to cry.

"We assured him Alexis wasn't here, but I'm not sure he believed us," he says.

"How'd he find you?" I ask.

"I don't know. My best guess is he got the rental car company to talk, and he traced me here since the car you rented under my name is in the garage," Cooper says. "He said he was going to your mom's place next."

Alexis makes a face. "I'm so sorry." I can tell how bad she feels.

"Hey, don't be," Cooper says to her. "We're fine. We threw him off the scent. He'll never find you where you are now, and I imagine Gregory was careful with the car he got you."

"I'd think so, too. I think he could outsmart my dad, anyway," Alexis says.

"Let's hope so," I mutter. "Thanks for the heads up."

"Stay safe out there, you two. We'll do what we can to distract him."

We hang up, and even though this place is all glass, I feel safe here. We're out in the middle of the desert alone. The nearest neighbor is an entire block away.

I don't think he'll find us here.

I pull Alexis into my arms. "You okay?" I ask softly.

"Yeah," she murmurs. "I feel good here. If we just hunker down the next two days, we should be fine."

I nod. "We *will* be fine."

"What if he finds us?" she asks.

I shrug. "What's the worst that will happen? So he finds us. And then he finds out we're married."

"And then he points out some clause in my contract that says I'm not allowed to get married or have a life of my own or run away, and he'll somehow find a way to ruin it like he ruins everything that's good in my life."

I pull her into me more tightly. "He won't ruin us, Alexis. I promise."

I really hope that's a promise I can keep.

Chapter 28
Alexis

The two days pass far too quickly for my liking. I try to savor every moment we have together as much as I can, but I feel the time slipping away.

He asked me what would be so bad about my dad finding us.

I told him I was worried he'd find some way to ruin us.

The truth is I'm not just *worried* about it. It's inevitable.

I'm sure there's some fine print in that old contract that says I'm not allowed to date somebody or marry somebody without his approval first. And which contract will win in the end? The one my father drew up when I was sixteen, or the government document marriage license I signed twelve years later?

I don't have proof there's anything of that nature in the contract, but I know my father.

Or at least…I thought I did.

I never thought he'd blackmail me into marrying Brooks, and he did.

I never thought he'd put his own interests before mine, and he did.

The thought occurred to me a few days ago, but I pushed it out.

Now, though, with just Danny and me in this quiet desert house moments bright and early before we're going to check out and make the two-hour trip for our honeymoon celebration day at Disneyland, I sit in front of the glass windows and stare out at the pool sunken within the brown landscape and the sparse cacti and sharp succulents as I analyze the whole situation.

I'm holding a hot cup of tea while I look outside, and I glance over at him as he slides onto the couch beside me. He slides a hand onto my thigh.

"Everything in the car?" I ask.

He nods. "Ready to go. You seem lost in thought. What are you thinking about?"

I lift a shoulder as I return my gaze out the window. "My dad. How strange this whole thing is. I feel like I'm missing something, but I can't put my finger on what."

"What do you mean?"

I blow out a breath. "Just…I don't know. I always figured he'd keep the company forever and then pass it down to me, and now I'm on the run from him because I don't want to be forced to marry someone I don't love."

"Did he say he would keep it forever?"

"Not in so many words, but I'm not sure why I would have thought that otherwise. He built it from the ground up, and aside from me, it's his pride and joy." My brows crinkle together as I try to fit the pieces together. "And then he just suddenly wants to merge with a management group? It doesn't make sense."

"Well, things change as life changes, right?" he points out. "Like us. Did you ever think you'd end up married to the bad boy of baseball?"

I glance over at him. "You really like that nickname, don't you?"

His lips tip up. "Yeah, I do. But seriously. Do you think maybe his priorities just changed?"

I shift my gaze back to the window. "Bodega Talent has been his main priority since my mother passed away. It's been eighteen years, Danny. It doesn't make sense that suddenly that would change overnight."

"Was it overnight, though? Or has this been brewing since he first started letting the world believe you were with Brooks?" His words are definitely something to consider.

"You think he's been planning this for the last four years?" I wonder.

"Maybe longer, and maybe Brooks is in on it, too. Maybe he's got something on your dad, and he's forcing this merger." He shrugs. "How did he initially set you up with Brooks?"

"My dad has been working with D-Three for years."

"D-Three?" he repeats.

"The Donovan's management company. The one we're merging with," I explain. "They've been my management company since the beginning, and Brooks has been my manager."

"Hm," he grunts.

"What?"

"Just seems…strange. Does your dad have money?"

I shrug. "We don't talk about his financials. I assume he's doing fine since he takes his cut on all of my deals plus everyone else he represents, but it's all handled by his business partners. Why?"

"Money makes people do strange things sometimes, that's all."

I nod. He's right, but I don't see my dad being in financial trouble. He has far too many clients for that to be the issue.

Unless he's right and Brooks has something to do with all this.

But I just don't see Brooks doing that, either. He's quiet and stoic, he lets me live my life, and he's a good manager who fades into the background most of the time.

I trust him…I think. Maybe I've been wrong this whole time. Maybe it's the quiet ones you have to watch out for.

"What does Brooks do for your career versus your dad?" he asks.

I take a sip of my tea before I answer. "My dad primarily handles performances and appearances. Management companies usually deal more with the career goal side of things, but since my father is so ingrained in my career, he does that part of that for me, too. Brooks tends to help with the musical production side of things—arranging recordings and making sure my band will be there, maintaining my schedule, things like that."

"And what advantages would this merger have for either side?"

I've been thinking about that, and mostly, it seems like it's financial advantages for the head honchos involved—my dad and Brooks's dad. "I guess the biggest advantage is that it would dominate the market since it's two huge companies coming together. A lot of money will exchange hands with this merger, and it's the businessmen who will benefit from it in the end as they cut some of the overhead costs. And it would create a conglomerate housed under one roof—a one-stop-shop for artists, which is attractive to people like me who have busy schedules."

"And the downsides?" he asks.

"Some artists might feel lost in the shuffle at such a big organization. Others might jump ship if they don't like one or the other company or the way the merger is handled. Apart from that…" I shrug. "That's about all I can come up with.

"So if this goes through, both men are set to make a shit ton of money and potentially might lose a few clients but will likely gain a hell of a lot more in the process?"

I nod. "That pretty much sums it up."

"Sounds like a no brainer, then. Maybe there's nothing fishy going on, and your dad just really wanted this to happen." He squeezes my thigh.

"I appreciate that you're giving him the benefit of the doubt," I say softly. "But I'm not sure he deserves it."

He leans over and presses a soft kiss on my cheek. "Either way, let's enjoy our last day on the run, shall we?"

I nod, and we leave this lovely house and head on toward our magical honeymoon day.

Chapter 29
Danny

We stop in a shop just outside the park to purchase our outfits for the day. It's against park rules to dress in full costume, but we get as much as we can to disguise our identities.

Alexis grabs a skin-colored t-shirt with a bikini on it along with a skirt that looks like a mermaid tail and a red wig to go as Ariel. I find a pirate hat with long braids sticking out of it, and when we get back to the car to change into our outfits, I borrow some of Alexis's eyeliner to really play the part.

We head into the park, disguised but not fully costumed, and Alexis is practically skipping as we make our way down Main Street. We pass through the castle and head right for Peter Pan's Flight, and we use our fast passes to cut the line so we can fit more rides in.

She squeals as we fly over London and Neverland at night, and we hold hands and laugh as we ride the carousel next.

We scream on the roller coasters, we get dizzy on the tea party ride, and we relax on the cruise.

We hold hands as we walk through the park, and we both feel like every other person here. We're just here for a magical day of fun, and we're having it.

We pause the fun for an early dinner, and it's as we're getting up from our Mickey ice cream bars that she freezes.

"What's wrong?" I ask.

She nods over toward where she's looking, and when I turn in that direction, I spot him.

Brooks.

"Shit," I mutter. "Come with me."

We run in the opposite direction toward It's a Small World, giving us a nice, long ride to hopefully lose them.

"How'd they track us here?" she asks softly. "We didn't tell anybody."

"No idea. Gregory's car, maybe?"

"Maybe," she murmurs. "Or your mom's credit card."

I wrinkle my nose. I bet she's right. "Do you want to stay or go?"

"I don't know." Her eyes are misty as she keeps her voice down so as not to raise suspicion of anyone else sitting on our boat with us. "I wish they'd just leave us alone. We'll be back tomorrow anyway."

"I'm sure he's just looking out for you," I say gently. "Maybe he wants to get in touch with you before the Christmas Eve performance."

"Maybe." She glances up at the little animatronics dancing beside us. "I don't want to leave, but we probably should."

"We can come back any time we want, Lex." I try to offer reassurance, but I know how stupid it sounds.

We have no idea if we can just come back.

Bases Loaded

Sure, we can put on disguises, and we can act like kids and run around holding hands...but we have no idea what any of this is going to look like after tomorrow.

As far as her father's concerned, she made a promise to marry Brooks, and who knows how far he'll go to force her to follow through on that promise.

Either way...I'll be there.

I have nowhere else to go, and he has no idea that she can't marry Brooks now since she's already married.

I blow out a heavy breath. "Then once this ride is done, we head out."

She nods, but her eyes tell the whole story. She's sad we have to leave.

I am, too.

"I have an idea," she says. "Can I look up something on your phone?"

I hand it over to her, and she types something in. "Nice. Less than a five-minute walk."

"What are we doing?" I ask.

"You'll see." She raises a brow and hands my phone back to me.

We stick to the crowds as we walk, carefully keeping watch for Brooks or her dad, and we make it out of the park without being detected. We follow the sidewalk around and then Alexis looks at the street signs and turns one way. I hold her hand as if I know where she's taking me, and a few minutes later, we stop in front of a shop with the words *Kingdom Ink* on the outside.

"Kingdom Ink?" I say.

She lifts a shoulder as she pulls open the door. "I've always wanted a tattoo."

My eyes widen. "You have?"

"Well, no. But I know you can't play ball with that ring on, and I thought it would be romantic to use our honeymoon day to get matching tattoos on our ring fingers."

My jaw slackens. "Are you serious?"

She lifts a shoulder. "Sure. Why not?"

"Uh, because I'm fucking terrified of needles?"

She laughs. "Toughen up, buttercup." She sinks into my chest, and I wrap my arms around her. "Will you do this with me?"

She doesn't really even need to ask. As her brown eyes meet mine, I know I will do anything just to see the question in her eyes melt into a smile.

"Of course I will."

I'm rewarded with that smile I adore so much, and that's when I ask my next question. "What are we getting?"

"I was thinking a D on the inside of my ring finger for me, an A on the inside for you."

I nod. "Deal. Let's do it."

We head inside, and it's not busy. The woman at the counter greets us and asks us how she can help.

"We'd like matching tattoos on our ring fingers," Alexis tells her.

She nods. "We have a hundred dollar minimum each, and Carl has an opening now if you'd like."

"Now's good," Alexis says.

I feel like I might puke, but this is for my wife.

"Now's great," I say brightly.

We're taken back and told to sit in a chair, and Alexis volunteers to go first. She slips off her ring and slides it onto the opposite hand. "I want a D right here," she says to apparently Carl, the artist covered in tattoos, pointing to the inside of her ring finger.

Bases Loaded

He gives her a look, and for just a second, I think he might recognize her. But he plays it cool if he does. The wig is definitely off-putting, anyway. "You won't be able to wear jewelry on it until it's fully healed," he says.

"What about up the side of my ring finger, like here?" she asks, running her pointer finger along the side of her ring finger that touches her middle finger when her fingers are together.

"You could leave your ring on for that," he says.

"I want it to say D-A-N-N-Y in tiny letters in a simple block script serif font."

My chest tightens.

She wants my name tattooed on her skin.

He shows us an example from his book, and she nods before she glances over at me.

"My whole name?" I ask.

"Yeah. Because it's forever, but also because I don't want anyone to think a random D on my finger means this is where you put your *dick*." She glances back at Carl. "Smaller than that, even. Just really simple and elegant."

"If it meant *dick*, you should put it on your mouth," I mutter.

"Danny!" she chides, and Carl laughs.

He glances over at me. "You?" he grunts.

"Same, but I want it to say A-L-E-X-I-S. Or should I get C-A-R-R-I-E?"

"Alexis," Carl repeats. He snaps his finger. "I knew who you were the second you walked in here. Why are you wearing a wig?"

"So I could slip into a tattoo shop undetected," she says dryly. "Are you a fan?"

"My daughter is. Sorry for blowing your cover. I won't tell anyone—except her if that's okay. Ready to get started?"

"That's okay." She nods. "And if you do a really good job, I'll blast your name on Instagram, okay?"

"You got it."

He does, in fact, do a really good job, and then it's my turn.

I noticed how much she was making a face like it hurt like hell while he did hers, and I sit in the chair for my turn.

I'm nervous. I settle on *Alexis* and I think about adding *Carrie* to the other side at a later time if it doesn't hurt too much.

It hurts like a motherfucking bitch.

But I've taken a ninety mile an hour baseball to the thigh. I can handle this pain.

I think about closing my eyes to bear the pain, but instead, my eyes meet hers.

She's looking at me with this pure adoration, and it's just one more moment that makes me feel like we're in this together.

It's a simple gesture, but it's beautiful. It's a reminder that even when I have to take off my ring, or she does, it doesn't matter. It's just a piece of hardware. But this is a permanent outward sign that'll go with us into the grave, and there's something simple and wonderful about that.

The tattoos are meant to last forever.

And so is our union.

We will figure out a way to make it work past these nine days.

We just have to face the first battle in less than twenty-four hours.

Chapter 30
Alexis

The pain was worth it for the beauty of the mark on my skin.

His is just as beautiful as mine, and as soon as it's had a few days to heal, we'll lock fingers together, sealing our names together.

I can't stop staring at it.

I can't stop staring at my ring, either.

It's beautiful, and I'm having a hard time believing all this is real.

But it is.

I don't know if I've ever been so giddy with happiness before in my life, and I've managed to put the end of it out of my mind for the last few days.

But we're running short on time.

We walk toward the condo where our rental is for the night—another one courtesy of Danny's mom, or maybe this one is courtesy of someone else so her credit card can't be traced.

It's in a big building, so it would be hard to pinpoint us. He left the car parked at the parking lot at Disneyland, so it's not like they'll track us down that way.

And we're less than an hour from where I need to be tomorrow night, so we'll head that way tomorrow.

We're standing in the kitchen just after we've gotten our luggage in, each of us on one side of a peninsula counter, and I've just taken off my Ariel wig when Danny's phone starts to ring. He flashes me the screen to show me it's Gregory calling, and he clicks *answer* and then the speaker button as he nods at me to take the call. He slides the phone across the counter.

"Hello?"

"Mrs. Brewer, hello," he says.

It's the first time someone has called me Mrs. Brewer.

I melt.

"I see you've checked in all right. Do you need anything?" he asks.

"We're fine now, thanks. But I will need help getting dressed and styled for tomorrow's performance," I say.

"I've thought of that, and I have someone picking up your dress from the house now. He'll drop it at a secure location, and tomorrow we'll send in stylists for you to the condo where you're staying now. They've been informed they'll be working on a celebrity, and they signed NDAs, so word won't get out until you're ready for it to. So, barring any other unforeseen circumstances, you will see your father when you step out of the limousine I've arranged for you tomorrow when you arrive at the red carpet event before your performance."

Tears pinch behind my eyes. "You really thought of everything," I murmur.

"I did. I will be in attendance should you need any additional security, though I think Mr. Brewer has been doing a fine job of keeping you safe in my absence."

He has, though he won't be able to forever. He'll have his own responsibilities to return to very soon, which means I'll need Gregory back.

I'll need him with me when I finish shooting the movie. I'll need him with me traveling to and from the studio as I record my next album, or on date nights out with my husband once we break the news to the media, or on any of a million other outings that he's always accompanied me to.

But what if he doesn't want to come back?

What if he's happy with Danny's mom and now I'm out one personal security guard I trust with my entire life?

How will I ever find anyone to replace him?

"Danny has been incredible, but we both know I'll need you back full-time starting tomorrow as soon as I step out of that limo," I say. "If nothing else, I might need your protection from my father and Brooks."

"Neither of them trusts me anymore, Mrs. Brewer. I'm not certain they'll welcome me back," he admits.

"Well, it doesn't matter. I'm welcoming you back. You're *my* employee, and as long as you want this job, it's yours."

"I appreciate that, ma'am," he says. "Oh, and Mr. Brewer?"

Danny glances up. "Yeah?"

"I've neutralized the threat."

Danny grins. "Good work, MacGyver."

"Thank you, sir."

"Don't *sir* me, Greg. If I'm going to call you Dad one day, you can't be calling me sir."

"We're a long way from that, Mr. Brewer. But thanks for the vote of confidence." The line goes dead, and Danny starts to laugh.

I glance up at him. "What's so funny?"

"He's a pretty cool dude." His eyes are twinkling, and I get the sense that he's really okay with his mom seeing Gregory—if that's in fact what's going on.

"Yeah, I like him too. But he *hates* when people call him Greg."

"Why do you think I do it?" He pauses, and his eyes are heated when they land on mine. "So, Mrs. Brewer, huh?"

"It's the first time I've heard it," I admit.

"I like the way it sounds," he says. "In fact, hearing it made me kind of horny."

"What doesn't make you horny?" I tease.

He chuckles. "You've got a point. Pretty much every time we are in the same room together or I think of you or I hear a song by you or I hear your name or I take a breath, I'm horny for you."

A thrill runs along my spine. "Right back at you, Mr. Brewer."

He raises a brow. "Really?"

"I don't have a lot of experience when it comes to this stuff, but I know what feels good, and it seems like every time I'm with you feels better than the last time."

"Well, then let's give ourselves a new challenge to overcome."

With those words, he darts around the counter and pulls me into his arms. His lips crash down to mine, and this kiss is intense and urgent as he proves his last statement true. His hips buck to mine, and he's hard and raring to go.

The ache between my legs intensifies as my own body prepares for the delicious pleasure he's about to give me.

He pushes my skirt up and slides my panties down my legs, and then he lifts me and perches me on the edge of the kitchen counter.

He shoves his way between my legs, and then he makes a meal out of me right there on the counter.

Bases Loaded

I lean back onto my palms, my chest pushing out into the air as if my breasts instinctively searching out his mouth even though it's hot on my pussy right now.

He hums against my wet, sensitive flesh as his tongue presses against my clit, the heat nearly unbearable as the onslaught of pleasure begins.

God, I love being Danny Brewer's wife.

Chapter 31
Danny

Christmas Eve morning is upon us, and I realize far too late I didn't buy my wife a gift.

I'm guessing she hasn't had time to get me one, either—and that's fine. I don't need anything except her.

Besides, the blow job she rewarded me with last night after I made her come on the counter was a pretty damn good gift, if I'm being honest.

We slept in mostly because we could, but that means we're wasting the day away. By the time we wake up, we only have a mere five hours until the stylists descend and start preparing her for tonight's event.

It's really only this morning that I realize she walked out on her wedding to one man and will be showing up at her first event afterward on the arm of another.

Publicly, I will look like *the other man* in this scenario. I will represent everything I hate when I think about my dad and how he took my childhood away from me, how at the young age of merely seven, my innocence was shattered.

And now I will appear to be doing the same thing.

I'm not...but it won't look that way.

Maybe we didn't think this through.

I don't care about my own reputation. I know what's real and what's going on here, and so do my mom and Anna, and that's all that matters.

But I care about her. I care about her brand. I care what her fans think. They may not support us if they support Brooks, and that's not something the two of us have ever really addressed.

She's nervous. She reviews her playlist. She sings Christmas songs, and I hum along in my off-key voice as she asks my opinions about things I know literally nothing about.

She's ready, and I think the nerves have far less to do with her performance than with seeing her father and her would-be husband tonight.

I do what I can to calm her nerves, but I get it. I'm nervous, too.

It doesn't feel like Christmas. We've done nothing to really prepare for the holiday ahead. I don't have a tree up in my house in Vegas. Hell, I've been on the run for the last nine days. I haven't even bought Christmas gifts for my mom or my sister. We should've celebrated the holiday when we were all together in Mission Beach. Instead, we were celebrating our wedding.

What a fucking whirlwind the last few weeks have been. It seems like Thanksgiving kicked off this tornado we were powerless to stop.

And now here we are, barreling toward the epic culmination of it all.

"Are you okay?" I ask softly as she finishes practicing a song and starts pacing.

"Not really."

Bases Loaded

"What will help?"

"Just getting it over with."

"It'll all be over in less than twelve hours," I say.

"Yeah, and then what? I hate the unknown. I hate the wondering. I hate the fear. I hate that all I want is to take control of my own life." She collapses on the couch beside me.

"You've gone a long way in making that happen, Lex." I hold up my ring finger where the silver glints in the light, and the redness from the tattoo I got just last night is starting to fade. "*We* have gone a long way. And I'm right here with you, holding your hand as we navigate this next part."

"I just keep thinking about my last Christmas with my mom. I was nine and didn't know what was coming just a few months later. I remember I was mad because I wanted these dumb dolls that really, looking back, were kind of slutty for a nine-year-old girl, and there weren't any under the tree. There were dozens of other gifts, and I should've been beyond happy, but I didn't get the one I wanted. I threw a big fit and ruined the entire morning, and it felt like it's what kicked off my dad coming down harder on me. I spent the entire day in my room without my presents until we had to leave to go to my aunt's house. This was back when we still lived in Nevada. And I cried and cried because it was the first time I felt like my dad was really mean to me. But looking back, he wasn't mean at all. He was teaching me that I can't throw a fit to get my way. And now I'm worried what lessons he's going to try to pull from all this." She shrugs a little at the end. "Am I just a nine-year-old throwing a fit?"

"Babe, those are two completely different situations. This isn't a nine-year-old throwing a fit. This is your adult *life*. This is your *happiness*," I point out.

"Yeah, but back then, I thought it was my life and my happiness, too. And now I look back and see how right he was.

Will I look back at this in twenty years and see how right he was?" she asks.

"Jesus Christ, no." It physically hurts my heart that she thinks that. "I wish I could give you the perspective you need to see that. He's controlling every aspect of who you are, including thoughts like these. You're smart, and you're talented, and you're incredibly capable, but he's trained you to rely only on him. You can rely on yourself, too, Lex. And me. Always me. But as much as I want you to do that, I also want you to see how very much you can stand on your own two feet. You may attribute a lot of your success to him, and maybe he was able to tug on the strings in the background to give you advantages others wouldn't have had, but ultimately, it's *you* who is your brand. It's *your* voice, *your* acting abilities, and *your* talents that have gotten you where you are, not his. It's *you* that I love, that your fans love, that has reached the astronomical levels of success you have."

I stand, and I pull her up with me.

She tosses her arms around me and holds me tight. "Thank you," she whispers into my chest. "I love you so much, Danny."

"I love you, too, baby. No matter what." I press a kiss to the top of her head, and she looks up at me with tears in her eyes.

"No matter what," she says resolutely.

We order brunch up to the room since we're in that strange time between breakfast and lunch. We shower together without getting frisky, and we get dressed and ready for the day. I shave again, though the shadow will be back when we arrive this evening.

We go through the motions carrying us toward this evening, the anticipation of what awaits us never really very far but still something we keep a tight lid on until we no longer can.

Chapter 32
Alexis

The stylists descend.

The dresses arrive. They're all pre-approved by my father, of course, but I get the final say for which one I want to wear tonight. It has to be red since I said I wanted red, and I slip into each one to take a look at how it fits as I realize I've gained a little weight since the last time I had to slip into a selection of dresses in my usual size. All the donuts and bacon and the lack of my regular dance routine is starting to catch up with me.

I select a sparkly dress in the end that I feel like a princess in. It's a V-neck with a tight bodice laced up in the back with a corset. It has a full, floor-length skirt, and it feels both festive and beautiful. The shoes that match it are six inches high, and it's a damn good thing I've practiced walking in heels because the fear of tripping and falling flat on my face is real.

As if I don't have enough to worry about.

We order in a light dinner before I finish getting ready.

My make-up is done to perfection. My hair is curled into gorgeous waves, secured partway back and out of my face with a beautifully sparkly holiday clip. I select the necklace and matching earrings that best compliment the gown.

The stylists leave, and Danny helps me slip into the gown.

He takes a step back and stares at me.

"How the fuck did I get so lucky?" he asks.

I glance down a little demurely. "I feel like I'm the lucky one."

He's wearing the tux he wore at our wedding, and we're ready to go.

"Gregory just texted me that the car is downstairs waiting for us. It'll let us out on the red carpet for the event. He's already there waiting." He clears his throat. "And, uh, so are your dad and Brooks."

I feel the color drain from my face. I mean, I knew they would be, so it's not a surprise. But knowing it's going to happen versus knowing they're there waiting for me *right now* is a little terrifying.

"I'm not ready," I cry. I know I shouldn't cry. My mascara might run. My make-up will be ruined. I'm television ready. This is a live event, and I have to maintain professionalism while also looking decent enough to appear on 4K and HD screens across the country where people can pick apart every single pore of my skin.

It's only now I realize how very much I've enjoyed my privacy over the last week or so.

"Hey, hey," he soothes, pulling me into his arms. "You're ready. We've got this. He can't do anything to you in front of the cameras, right? It'll be fine."

It'll be fine. His words echo in my head.

I love the sentiment, but I don't know how he can guarantee that.

He *can't* guarantee that.

Bases Loaded

I wish he could, but he can't. This feeling that my dad is going to do something tonight surges over me.

People will be watching. This is one of the biggest events of the season, and I know all eyes will be on me. Word was out I was missing, and even though I assured them I was fine in my Instagram post, people will see the ring on my finger. They'll see the tattoo on my hand, though I typically hold the microphone in my right hand, not my left. They'll analyze every detail just as they always do—the designer of the dress, the shoes, the hair clip, the jewelry. Who did my hair, my make-up. It wasn't my regular team, and stock for these designers and stylists will shoot up because I used them.

I'm done being the unknown girl walking down the street in the sunshine with her new husband. I'm done being the new secret Mrs. Brewer.

I'm back to being Alexis Bodega, America's Pop Princess.

But I kind of fell in love with the life I had with Danny over the last nine days.

I don't want to let any of this go. I'm not ready.

If there was some guarantee we'd escape this unscathed, I'd jump at it. But there isn't, and life will return to how it's always been in a few hours.

I wasn't happy in my old life.

But in this one…I am.

I drag my feet over toward the door. He clutches my hand, and he sets his on the door handle to let us out of our condo.

I set my hand on his arm before he opens it, squeezing it tightly, and he freezes.

"Danny, promise me something," I say desperately.

He turns around to look at me, his eyes so full of sincerity and love that it's overwhelming. "Anything," he breathes.

"Promise me that whatever happens tonight, we're going to be okay."

His eyes soften as they fall on me, and he tilts his head a little. "I promise."

The authenticity of his words gives me the tiny measure of comfort I needed.

I nod. "Okay. Then let's go."

People stare as we exit the lobby. I hear my name. *Oh my God, that's Alexis Bodega! Who's that man with her? Is that Danny Brewer?*

He clutches my hand tightly in his. He isn't used to this level of attention, and this is our first public appearance—which isn't really all that public considering it's not hundreds of flashbulbs going off in our faces all at once like it will be when we step out of the limo on the other side of all this.

We slip into the car waiting for us, and we jet off toward Los Angeles.

It's over an hour with traffic before we arrive, and Danny texts Gregory that we're here. He flashes me the screen when he receives a response.

Gregory: *I've been in touch with your driver. He knows what to do.*

We're here. The driver pulls up to the curb at the start of the red carpet.

The door on Danny's side opens, and he slides out before I do. He reaches his hand in to help me out of the car.

I slide over on the leather seats, the full skirt of my gown tripping me up a little, and I set one of my six-inch heels down onto the carpet that extends down into the street for my arrival. Danny helps me out of the car, and flashbulbs blink at us, blinding us as we're photographed publicly for the first time.

I set my other foot on the carpet, too, and I use Danny's hand to help pull me up out of the car, the flashbulbs continuing to blind me as the paparazzi gathered here are relentless.

But there's a short break between flashes, and that's when my eyes find Brooks first. And standing beside him is my father.

TO BE CONCLUDED IN BOOK 5, GRAND SLAM

Alexis's father tells me he's going to ruin me. He does not want his pop star daughter or her brand associated in any way with the bad boy of baseball.

I make it my mission to prove to her father that I'm not the bad guy he thinks I am. But he takes things a few steps too far, causing major issues that will affect my upcoming baseball season.

It's going to take a grand slam to make everything right again, but I will not give up on the woman I've fallen for.

Acknowledgments

I'll save my acknowledgments for the final book! I can't wait for you to see what's coming next...

xoxo,
Lisa Suzanne

About the Author

Lisa Suzanne is an Amazon Top Ten Bestselling author of swoon-worthy superstar heroes, emotional roller coasters, and all the angst. She resides in Arizona with her husband and two kids. When she's not chasing her kids, she can be found working on her latest romance book or watching reruns of *Friends*.

Also by Lisa Suzanne

HOME GAME

Vegas Aces Book One
#1 Bestselling Sports Romance

CURVEBALL

Vegas Heat: The Expansion Team
Book One

Made in United States
Orlando, FL
08 April 2024